In 1990, readers were charmed by the exploits of E. P. Rizzoli, the hero of Mark Ciabattari's *Dreams of an Imaginary New Yorker Named Rizzoli*. Now the Felliniesque character is back, with a whole new set of dreams. In *The Literal Truth,* Rizzoli dreams of seeing hanging "strings of memories" alive with tiny New Yorkers, and of being forced to make love with a phantom femme fatale. That metropolitan chore, alternate side of the street parking, assumes new meaning the day Rizzoli dreams that his car has a will of its own during the hours it must be moved.

Advance Praise for *The Literal Truth: Rizzoli Dreams of Eating the Apple of Earthly Delights*:

"Quirky, engaging stuff—there's a genuine feel for New York streets, a sharp eye at work, and a fine backhanded logic."
—Nik Cohn, author of *The Heart of the World*

"I love my life in New York since I read *The Literal Truth.* Whenever I encounter a particularly intransigent knot of urban insanity, I try to imagine what Rizzoli would make of it. I smile more because that unassumingly sane everyman is out on these streets with me."
—Barbara Garson, author of *MacBird!* and *Security*

"A marvelous book revealing the universal in the dreams of Rizzoli—a one-of-a-kind character who combines humor, fantasy, and social satire in the style of a modern-day Swift."
—Janice Eidus, author of *Vito Loves Geraldine* and *Urban Bliss*

"*The Literal Truth* is witty stuff, trenchant and sly. We could recognize ourselves in the remarkable, foolish antics of his characters. Mark Ciabattari knows all too well exactly where we live. When Rizzoli dreams, he dreams us."
—Anthony Brandt, author of *The People Along the Sand*

What the critics said about Mark Ciabattari's *Dreams of an Imaginary New Yorker Named Rizzoli*:

"Rizzoli is an anxious anti-hero . . . an urban everyman. [His] . . . funny . . . satirical vignette-like dreams [show] the influence of media on our perceptions [and] point to our mediated lives, to commercials that advertise instant love as ardent strangers pursue each other with flowers." — *The New York Times Book Review*

"A collection of funny-frightening pieces dealing with the extraordinary life of an everyman . . . called Rizzoli in a really mad, mad world." — *Associated Press*

"Ciabattari . . . brims with brio in this fanciful, cannily humorous look at the jungles of darkest Manhattan." — *Publishers Weekly*

"These twenty-one surreal parables of city life [are] part Beckett, part Woody Allen. . . . Rizzoli [is] a hapless New Yorker who acts out his hopes and fears on a nightmarish cityscape that bears an only slightly skewed relation to the real Manhattan." — *Kirkus Reviews*

"Ciabattari's art and wit are everywhere present in his character's dazzled and frazzled psyche. . . . Hip, young New Yorkers will find what . . . Ciabattari offers is fresher, funnier and more fearsome [than] brat-pack fiction." — *Booklist*

"Twenty-one postmodern vignettes . . . of a New York everyman named Rizzoli [who] fights the odds in this crazy city armed with nothing but a shield of dreams." — *New York Newsday*

"Ciabattari has a knack for taking the mundane to the metaphysical level and pushing the human experience to unbearable limits. . . . [Rizzoli] has pathos, humor and a common touch." — *The Montana Standard*

"Displacement and depersonalization are the dark themes that lurk behind what otherwise might read as playful witty fantasies. . . . The dreams of this imaginary Rizzoli—a quintessential New Yorker—read like the anxious daydreams to which New Yorkers might be prone while packed into rush hour subways or endlessly waiting in line somewhere for something. They speak to the storms and stress peculiar to a day in the life of this city [and] range in tone from Woody Allen to Kafka."

—*Street News*

"A montage of sketches [about] a surreal but familiar New York City. Some of the dreams are whimsical, some fantastic, a few are simultaneously frightening and funny. Ciabattari . . . reveal[s] a keen ear for dialogue and a sharp eye for telling detail."

—*The Ontario Whig-Standard*

"An original humorous fantasy . . . of [sometimes] frightful beauty . . . where New York is transformed into a type of surreal Disneyland."

—*Il Giorno* (Milan)

"Ciabattari . . . has knowingly put together . . . the humor . . . [of] slapstick . . . [and] a rhythm associated with fine cinematic montage. . . . With the nervous vitality central to the literary myth of New York."

—*Il Messaggero* (Rome)

"Pyrotechnic mode of expression . . . transforms the metropolis into a type of sky painted by Chagall where the figures fly upward and our Rizzoli assumes the dress now of Chaplin, now of the predictable Woody Allen."

—Alberto Bevilacqua, author of *La Califfa*

"This surreal fantasy . . . returns you to a Melvillian precedent [with Rizzoli] . . . the descendant of the strange . . . Bartleby, a personage who takes refuge in the dream." —*La Stampa* (Turin)

"Rizzoli [is the] emblem of Everyman in the ludicrous New York nightmare. . . . Rizzoli . . . owes something to . . . Chaplin's Tramp. . . . Ciabattari, . . . the dreamer of [Rizzoli], owes something to such predecessor pilgrims as Kafka and Ionesco."

—*New York Daily News*

The Literal Truth

Also by Mark Ciabattari

Dreams of an Imaginary New Yorker Named Rizzoli

The Literal Truth

Rizzoli

Dreams of

Eating the

Apple of

Earthly

Delights

....

Mark
Ciabattari

Canio's Editions

Sag Harbor, New York

"Birth and Rebirth in the Ever-Expanding Metropolis" first appeared in the
Winter 1991 issue of *Story*.

This book is a work of fiction. Names, characters, places, and incidents either
are the product of the author's imagination or are used fictitiously, and any
resemblance to actual persons, living or dead, events, or locales is entirely
coincidental.

Published in the United States by Canio's Editions, P.O. Box 1962, Sag Harbor,
NY 11963.

Library of Congress Catalog Card Number: 94-70904

ISBN: 0-9630164-7-4

Editor: Trent Duffy
Designer: Jessica Shatan
Production Managers: Trent Duffy/Jeanne Palmer

10 9 8 7 6 5 4 3 2 1

First Edition

Acknowledgments

My gratitude and appreciation to my wife, Jane, who shares the writer's life; to my son, Scott; and to the following special friends for their continued inspiration: Judith Goldschmidt, Canio Pavone, Jeanine Johnson Flaherty and the late Joe Flaherty, George Leeson, Ricki Winter, Ron Nowicki, Bob and Marvis Stoecker, Paul De Angelis, Helene Aylon, Daniel Walkowitz, Anna Villenchitz, George and Saundra Segan Wheeler and the Claude Monet Group.

My special thanks to the Virginia Center for the Creative Arts and its director, Bill Smart, for giving me the opportunity to write much of this work, and to the Italian publisher Leonardo Mondadori, for first bringing it to European readers, and to the Franz Kafka Center of Prague for recognizing it.

New York City.
July 6, 1994.

— To Anna —
a lifelong friend with
whom we have had
a lifetime of memories
All the best, with love
LIBO —

[New York City] can destroy an
individual or it can fulfill him,
depending a good deal on luck.
　—E. B. WHITE

While we are asleep in this
world, we are awake in another
one; in this way every man is
two men.
　—JORGE LUIS BORGES

Contents

Minor
Frustrations
in a Major City

Apropos of
Fighting
the Scarf

....

T he sky is wintry overcast as Rizzoli dreams he's in the backseat of a taxi stopped in traffic on Eighth Avenue in the Thirties, headed uptown. Outside, it's cold, windy. Out the window, left, he sees the gargantuan, two-block-long General Post Office with its elongated stairs leading up to the front of grayed marble columns stretching in a foreboding row. Rizzoli has the thought the building would please Kafka as, then, he turns to glimpse out the other window at Madison Square Garden. He thinks of Knicks' games he's been at inside there, jammed in with New York's wild basketball fans, sweating and hollering.

The traffic moves; his taxi travels quickly now and out the window up ahead, Rizzoli suddenly sees a huge Pendleton shirt billboard covering the east wall high up on the exposed red brick of an old, tall office building. The advertisement shows a red muffler standing on its end, eight feet tall. This muffler has a soft, silk-clad man draped around it; the man's arms neatly folded over his legs cinch in the muffler a few feet down from

3

the top. Behind the muffler, a ski lift shows in the background. In bold lettering, it says, "Try a Rizzoli for Style on a Winter Day."

He glances down to notice for the first time that with his black overcoat he is wearing a red muffler that is eight feet long and drapes over his knees in two streamers onto the floor.

It punches him in the stomach.

On this cold, sunny late winter day, Rizzoli dreams that he's standing as a street performer on SoHo's most celebrated corner, where he can look catty-corner to Dean & DeLuca's food emporium while his back is to the downtown annex of the Guggenheim Museum. He's blowing a slender flute as all eight feet of his red muffler lie in coils on the sidewalk. As the flute music plays, one end of the muffler begins to rise and sway to the music.

As that end rises higher to the music of Rizzoli's flute, and higher still, a young man with a gold ring in his nose passes by, not even glancing at the muffler.

Rizzoli plays on as that end rises higher and higher until all eight feet of muffler are straight up, slowly undulating.

Slowly the muffler begins wrapping itself like a muffler around Rizzoli's neck. With the music still playing, the muffler settles down, but not before one end flings itself over Rizzoli's back to make him look like a poet.

Then it begins strangling him. Downtown people pass by, feigning not to notice. Rizzoli's face grows redder, as red as the muffler. Even so, he manages to whisper, "Chickenshit muffler."

The muffler lets him loose.

On this gusting, early spring day, Rizzoli is walking downwind down Broadway, carrying two bags from Zabar's: one with his Nova, bagels, onions, cream cheese; the other with the seltzer.

Crossing 80th, Rizzoli suddenly notices a two-foot portion of his muffler is loose underneath his overcoat and flapping between his two bags. Forgetting everything, Rizzoli begins struggling to clasp his muffler back inside his coat. The grocery bag under his right arm drops and the bottles of seltzer smash, the water running onto the sidewalk. His other bag upends and spills. The Nova lays in a schmear of cream cheese on the dirty pavement. A laugh rings out from somewhere. Rizzoli is embarrassed by his predicament.

Calmly letting the muffler end flap away, he reaches into his pocket. With clenched lips, he mutters the threat, "I'm not fooling. You red mutha . . . Embarrass me in public and I'll . . . I'll . . ." Rizzoli holds the two-foot portion of his muffler, says, "I'm not fooling," and cuts it off with a pair of scissors.

"That'll show this muffler."

Rizzoli strolls up Park Avenue with the now only six-foot-long muffler wrapped once around his neck on the outside of his black overcoat. After leaving the Helmsley Building, after coming from Grand Central through the lobby of the MetLife Building, Rizzoli is midblock to 47th headed into a strong spring wind blowing and swirling down Park.

The cut end of his muffler starts flapping. Trying to grab on to it, Rizzoli nearly lets loose the other end. The flapping end snaps in the wind, hitting him in the eye.

"This red son-of-a-bitch . . . I'll get this woolly son-of-a-bitch if it kills me," Rizzoli utters, while the flapping end, whipped by the strong wind, strikes again.

"MUTHA BASTARD!" Rizzoli screams.

Rizzoli lunges out, grasping the muffler and falling so as to smother it under him. Lying there wriggling, he struggles to hold down the agitated muffler and at the same time undo his overcoat to wrap around the muffler.

Passersby occasionally raise their eyebrows to one another,

but no one stops the whole time Rizzoli lies writhing and screaming, "THIS RED BITCH AIN'T GONNA GET AWAY FROM ME." But he can't get his coat around the muffler.

Finally, in desperation, Rizzoli changes tactics. Underneath him, he grabs both wriggling ends and ties the muffler in one knot, then another and another and another until it feels like a giant knitting ball under him. It is finally quiet.

Rizzoli carefully pulls away, his hands still clutching the balled-up muffler. Once he sees it is helpless, he stands and quickly bowls the ball of red muffler out into the heavy traffic.

The first car misses it; Rizzoli cheers as the next car runs squarely over it. "PUNCH ME NOW, YOU BASTARD!" Other cars mash it down farther into the pavement as Rizzoli screams, "STRANGLE ME NOW, SHITHEAD!"

A Tiny Fragment
of the Ongoing
Forget-Me-Not
Experience

....

Spring. The day is sunny and brisk; the trees have first buds as Rizzoli dreams he is on the outside looking in through a street-level window at a strange scene. Inside, he sees a room as bare as a ballet studio with thin ropes, like cords from Venetian blinds, hanging down everywhere from the very high ceiling to within nine or ten feet of the varnished wooden floor. On each rope, climbing up and down, he sees what look like *No, it can't be. Little humans? Shinnying up and down? No.* He presses closer and squints. That's what it looks like to Rizzoli. Little four-inch-high humans.

New Yorkers? Are they little New Yorkers? Rizzoli can't tell for sure but he thinks they must be. Here he sees a little Greek waiter, wearing black pants and black vest and white shirt. Over there a little uniformed doorman. A tiny homeless person. And in the little fur there. *An East Side matron? Maybe.* All are real on that tiny scale and Rizzoli marvels at how easily they can all shinny on their ropes.

"Hey, buddy. You make anything out of this?" Rizzoli hears

a guy's voice say on his right. Rizzoli turns and sees another New Yorker who has also been standing and peering in intently. The guy is pointing inside. Rizzoli smiles and shrugs. The other guy shrugs back, turns away and again peers inside.

Rizzoli peers in again. Now it comes to him that the room inside is the fencing school on 71st and he's on the spot on the sidewalk outside where he often stops to watch two swordsmen in a mock duel. He steps back from the window to check if it is the right block. It is. *Between Columbus and Broadway.* He sees "Fencing School" on the closed doors.

He steps up to the window again, peers in and sees the little people scurrying up and down the ropes. *Where are the fencers?*

The other guy says something. Rizzoli turns to hear what and sees the other's pudgy face has an astonished look. "One is me," he says.

"What?" Rizzoli asks. He thought he heard "One is me" but that makes no sense. "Huh?"

"ONE IS ME," the guy repeats. "SEE IF ONE IS YOU."

"What? What? On the ropes?" Rizzoli points inside.

The guy nods.

Rizzoli peers back in, really intently now. He searches and then sees himself in miniature clinging to a rope in this near corner. He sees a stunning resemblance. *My little guy is me to the T,* Rizzoli thinks as he carefully studies the features of his little guy, who is stopped motionless midway on his rope. *Even down to the wire frame eyeglasses.*

Is my little guy dead? Rizzoli wonders. *Or what? He's so still and his eyes are closed shut.*

"One is me," Rizzoli says to the other guy. "Is yours (*dead?*) sleeping? Mine's sleeping."

"Mine, too," the other guy says. "Don't know what to make of it. Mine hasn't moved."

Rizzoli is relieved. Rizzoli sees about half the little humans are moving on their ropes and about half are still but he is glad the other guy's isn't moving either.

Just then inside the fencing school, Rizzoli sees the back door open and through it walks an old woman wearing a gray cape with a large cowl pulled up over her head. He's unable to see her face.

"Whatta we got here?" the other guy hollers. "Who's she?"

"You got me," Rizzoli says with a shrug.

He shrugs back.

Rizzoli peers back in and watches as the woman looks up at all the ropes hanging down with the little humans clinging to them. *Is she shaking her head at them?* Rizzoli can't be sure. He thinks so.

As she slowly circles, glancing up, Rizzoli notices that some little guys, who were very active all along, are now sliding down to the very ends of their ropes about four feet above her head. *What's this now?* Some of the little guys have started shaking their fists at her.

Not my little guy. He's still sleeping. Is he dead? Rizzoli sees there are even more little guys shaking their fists at her now.

The old woman suddenly hauls a broom out from under her cape. Rizzoli hollers out, "My GOD!" as she swings wildly back and forth at little humans who scurry up their ropes. Finally her broom swats a little fireman down onto the floor where he lies writhing. Then she starts trying to beat him to death with the broom handle.

Rizzoli and the other guy pound the window outside but the woman is oblivious. A blow hits square and the little fireman lies still. As she moves toward his body, Rizzoli hears, "HEY. OUR LITTLE GUYS ARE AWAKE! BUT WHAT ABOUT THIS KILLER WOMAN?"

Rizzoli looks up the rope and sees his little guy is awake and watching the old lady as she carefully sweeps the fireman's tiny body into her dustpan. Rizzoli is anxious about this whole inside scene now. *Watching that, what's my little guy thinking? Does he know who the woman is? Is he afraid it could happen to . . .* His little guy moves. Rizzoli loses his train of thought . . . *to,* . . . *to* . . .

Inside, his little guy darts up the rope. Outside, Rizzoli automatically remembers something important—about his WASP friend from work, Cheswick—that he's totally forgotten for the past five years or more. *It was Cheswick I deliberately lied to, not Shadely, and it makes all the difference. I must remember this.*

Inside, his little guy goes another quick shinny up the rope and stops. Outside, Rizzoli recalls instantly an episode he's totally blanked out for at least two years—after he first started dating his now longtime love, Phoenicia, he had also secretly dated Phoenicia's best friend and then rommmate for a short time, *Clarisse? Clarisse. Then I knew it was Phoenicia.*

So, now that it's come back to me, do I tell Phoenicia? Clarisse's moved out to California. Still . . .

Pondering this dilemma, Rizzoli absently watches as the dangling little humans parry one on one with the woman. Swaying daringly near her upraised broom, each one taunts her to swing. She stalks, swings and misses.

Now Rizzoli sees his little guy abruptly slide back down and as he does, Rizzoli's newly recalled memories begin fading automatically, leaving only traces. Rizzoli vows to remember what he just recalled. About Cheswick. About *Clara? Clara.*

His little guy stops four feet from the end of his rope and remains still. Outside, Rizzoli regains presence of mind. Immediately, he is alarmed that since his little guy is down that far he will get knocked off and killed by the woman, who has begun swinging wildly again.

Rizzoli watches in terror as his little guy slides to the end and dodges broom swing after broom swing.

One little guy falls. She clubs. He's dead. It's the outside stranger's little guy.

Rizzoli glances over at the other New Yorker. "Hey. You all right?" Rizzoli asks, not knowing for sure what effect this might have on him. "YOU ALL RIGHT?"

"Me?" asks the other guy, coming over to Rizzoli. "Listen, the way I figure it, the tiny me is dead. The big me is alive. It could be worse. Sure, that little guy was keeping some memories alive. Now those memories are gone forever. So, you win some. You lose some."

Rizzoli doesn't know how to respond. So, he shrugs. The other guy shrugs, says, "Who knows? WHO KNOWS?" and walks off down 71st toward Broadway.

Rizzoli can't bear to peer back in to see if his own little guy will be knocked off so he starts off in the opposite direction down 71st toward Columbus. As he walks, Rizzoli tries to recollect the important forgotten memories that he has just recalled at the window. He can't. He wonders if he's just forgotten or if this means his little guy has just been killed. He races back to the window.

What? Rizzoli wonders, seeing an apartment building where the fencing school was. He stops an old man, asks and is told by the man there hasn't been a fencing school in that building for at least twenty years.

The Image's Sexual Obsession Finds a Real Object

....

Saturday night, way late past midnight, sometime, Rizzoli is up on his high-riding platform bed, lying awake next to his true love, Phoenicia, who's fallen asleep. The blanket is off her and, in the pitch dark, he senses her form, her fully rounded hip under his white shirt, her bare legs pulled up. Her delicate perfume is faint in this still night of late spring.

Leaning over, he very gently pulls her blanket up so she won't get cold in the night and, while doing so, he glimpses dimly the top of the bookshelf with her red cabaret shoes (*the shoes!*) next to the Summer Preview issue of *New York* and, lying on this, the open case of the rented video, *Damage,* they had seen earlier on the little TV in the bedroom.

Rizzoli lies back comforted—and so pleased she decided to stay over at his place tonight. As he floats high up on his pillow, his mind drifts back to earlier this evening when he and Phoenicia had rented *Damage* because they both remembered its love scenes were so erotic the first time they'd seen it. They'd wanted to see it again to be put in the mood to make love.

When viewing the movie this second time, Rizzoli thinks of how they'd endured the now seemingly slow pace of the developing plot—how young, beautiful Anna (*slightly crazy from the start . . . the "damaged" one*) begins an obsessive love affair with her soon-to-be father-in-law, Stephen, a proper Englishman and member of Parliament who falls hopelessly and tragically in love with her.

With my Fast Forward broken . . . it was slow getting to that first love scene, Rizzoli recalls, the one he and Phoenicia had awaited eagerly. Finally, the movie had Anna phoning Stephen's office and at the sound of her voice—a stranger he's only recently met—Stephen whispers, "What's your address? I'll be there in an hour."

Then the scene at her London flat . . . Rizzoli sees it unfold again, as Stephen enters the flat to see Anna's on the bed drawing him to her (*his female fantasy*), their making love, wordlessly tangled in passion there and then across a glossy wooden floor and standing up in a doorway.

Watching these scenes unfold, he had begun kissing Phoenicia's ear, cheek, mouth. *Phoenicia, oh . . .* As Stephen and Anna groaned and tore at each other, he and Phoenicia had entwined slowly, intensely—and mutually. With their passions mounting like alternating movements of a symphony, building powerfully—oblivious to the movie by then—they had grasped each to the other until, at once, together, they came. As the movie lovers lay there exhausted, Rizzoli thinks, *we lay here kissing and kissing. It was perfect.* Lying, hearing her softly breathing next to him in the blackness, he thinks, *I've never loved anyone like I love Phoenicia.*

Reaching out, he strokes Phoenicia's soft shoulder very gently. She responds, awake, too, turning toward him. His hand moves down from her shoulder to touch her full breast. She reaches up to his face and pulls him to her mouth. His hand moves down across her taut stomach, as they kiss, pressing together.

Heat. Fire. It is happening again; here in the wordless, sightless dark, he feels sensations: her body writhing against his skin, his flesh becoming one with hers.

Her breathing grows louder until she moans. She squirms and moans louder and louder. So frenzied is her passion, Rizzoli is taken aback, he's never before experienced her in quite this fashion. Her sexuality is powerful but he didn't know until this instant, Phoenicia's sexuality was *this powerful. Her mystery . . . this great, . . . so primal . . . so driving.*

"I am what you desire." Rizzoli is sure he hears Phoenicia say this line of Anna's from the movie; probably, he thinks, because she's now throwing in a little erotic play from the movie. Going along, he cries out loud Stephen's initial question, "Anna, please . . . talk to me. Who are you?"

"I am what you desire." He hears Phoenicia say once more *in a voice even imitating Anna's.*

Now he hears Phoenicia saying something very different, "Suss-ANNA? Who is this SUSS-ANNA you're talking to . . . ?"

SUSS-ANNA?

". . . Is she some other woman? No! Rizzoli. Who?"

SUSS-Anna? Rizzoli feels Phoenicia pull back. He wants to explain but his words are inflected with the lust of the movie. Its words are running riot in his head and pouring out his mouth as *Stephen's? Not Stephen's.*

"Anna." *Dammit.*

"Oh, Anna." (*No.*) "Anna!"

"Who are you, Anna?"

Phoenicia is more upset. Rizzoli feels terrible to have hurt her so. *NO!* And he's stunned at the words still coming from his mouth intended for the video's Anna who, he thinks, *wants to lock me into her . . . blind? . . . obsession. And replace Phoenicia. No! No!*

14

"Anna," Rizzoli cries out.

Phoenicia leaps from the bed and grabs her red cabaret shoes as Rizzoli, a lust of *Damage* words still coming forth, is twisted on the bed seized up in the grip of the phantom lover, Anna. *GODDAMMIT!* He wrestles to get loose.

She grips him tighter, wrestling him this way and that to go on making love to him. He struggles to keep her from doing it. *No way this video whacko's going to make me her real-life male fantasy! If this phantom thinks I'm her real male fantasy object, this phantom's got another thought coming. . . .* Her invisible body pounding at him, he resists . . . *goddamn whacko.* She goes on twisting him to make love to her.

Exiting to the other room, Phoenicia closes the bedroom door nearly shut as Rizzoli is strenuously coupling with this phantom. He wants to get loose, but she contorts him into a writhing tangle that brings him pain.

Phoenicia! . . . "Anna." He tries to stop saying what she wants him to say. He can't. "Anna. Oh, Anna . . ." *No. NO!*

"Rizzoli," he hears Phoenicia's voice say through the door, which is open a crack so he can see she's dressed in her blue jeans, cabaret shoes, man's hat—so sexy in the shoes he loves and his old fedora. *Phoenicia, wait! . . . Wait,* Rizzoli's mind implores as the invisible Anna keeps pounding away at him.

Screw me over, . . . you'll regret it! Rizzoli struggles against Anna, who now seems to be lying back on the desk pulling him toward her.

"Rizzoli . . ."

Phoenicia.

". . . I want you to tell me. Who is Suss-anna?"

Suss? . . . -Anna. Rizzoli wants to explain desperately but the phantom woman pulls him closer. *No you don't . . . goddammit!* He pushes against her, wrestling the air, as she pulls him to her.

"Please . . . tell me who she is . . . before I go."

Silence.

Rizzoli is occupied to the full trying to stop this phantom coupling him. He's frightened to suddenly realize Anna's force *has to come from her video image having to steal a few moments of real sex. That's why her . . . desperate abandon, her not letting me go.* Her going on making love to him has Rizzoli beside himself.

"Rizzoli . . ."

He can't imagine what Phoenicia might think were she to throw the door open this instant and see him here doing the wild thing all by himself.

"Rizzoli, I'm leaving."

No, Phoenicia . . . "Anna."

His apartment door slams.

He struggles to keep from being destroyed further by this all-consuming passion of the "damaged" Anna's now misplaced obsession.

He hears Phoenicia's red shoes (*the red shoes!*) echoing down the flights of stairs.

Arching his back, he strains away from Anna, who pounds away and strains to draw him closer. The passionate words she wants him to say to her, he tries to keep locked inside by keeping his mouth clamped shut.

"Anna," he murmurs. *Still?* "Anna."

While she's strenuously coupling at him now, Rizzoli thinks how he feels nothing but fury *at the phantom,* and how his real love is *for Phoenicia always,* and to whom he's always been faithful. For this Anna he feels only the cold unreality of her video image.

But, when is this whacko Anna going to quit . . . screwing me? He can't think of when he's ever had sex like this where *I'm not listened to . . . have no say.*

The outside door to his building clanks shut. As Phoenicia starts down the street, going away, Rizzoli notices the lid is up on the plastic video case. He snaps the case shut. Anna's words for him stop and her grip on him vanishes. He's back to normal.

Down his block Phoenicia's footsteps are echoing. How can he ever explain to Phoenicia, he wonders, exhausted from his bout *with the sex obsession this Anna misplaced when she got loose from . . . her video cage. . . .*

Video cage?

"VIDEO CAGE?"

Getting
Away for
the Weekend

Nature's Order
Discovered
in a Walk
Near Montauk

....

A glorious Saturday morning. Not even eight o'clock yet and the coming-to-be summer sun is warm. The sky is cloudless and the sea calm. The sheer beauty of this place. Rizzoli can't believe it. The hills, dunes, the salt marsh, this path here along the pond and the sandy beach stretching on.

"What's special," Rizzoli remembers his East Hampton host and friend, Cheswick, telling him, Rizzoli, the weekend guest, "is this place out in the dunes; it's so remote, so secluded, you aren't going to know you're anywhere near the Fashionable Hamptons."

Cheswick is right, Rizzoli thinks. *This place is incredible.* Still, he's not fully engaged; he thinks, *there's something important I'm forgetting I have to do.*

He's impatient. He looks overhead and sees a flock of birds flying. *In a strange formation. No V. What the . . . ?*

He looks down and fumbles in his left pocket to see if he may have made a list to remind himself of whatever it is he thinks he's forgotten to do.

He finds a folded piece of paper in his left pocket, which he removes and opens. It's a list but he doesn't recognize it as his. *It's somebody else's? These are my g's, . . . but the t's and a's are not mine. Strange . . .* He reads,

To Do
1. See flock of starlings?? flying in infinity formation. ∞

He looks skyward again and sees it is infinity. He finds himself checking it off.

√1. See flock of starlings?? flying in infinity formation. ∞

There are other things on this list but before he can see what's second, he jams it back into his left pocket. He's impatient with this list; there's something else altogether more important he's forgotten. *What?* He stops and ponders, shading his eyes from the sun.

As he stands in place, the dune shifts and he looks down and sees its sand surging up, already burying his feet and rising higher. In seconds it's up to his calves, then his knees. He can't move, he's stuck. He fumbles in his left pocket, takes out the list and reads:

2. See the "Walking Dunes."

The dune is up to his mid-thighs as Rizzoli checks it off and peevishly wads up the list and jams it back into his pocket. The dune shifts and its sand ebbs off in another direction, freeing him.

Rizzoli continues along this path beside the pond through the marsh grasses and over little running brooks, while he tries to recall what it was he set out to do in the first place.

A loud flapping sound overhead startles Rizzoli, who looks skyward toward the beautiful azure blue and sees a huge brown and white bird. *Wingspan of six or seven feet, must be.*

He pulls out the list so he can check this off and reads:

3. See osprey.

Osprey? Rizzoli puzzles over, *What is an osprey?* and thinks the bird itself looks more like an extinct species from the age of dinosaurs. He checks it off anyway and then jams the list into his opposite pocket, the right one, by mistake.

Inside this pocket, he feels another slip of paper. He takes it out. *This is my list.*

He tosses the first list away and the wind carries it tumbling up and over the dunes.

Now Rizzoli is sure. *That first list didn't have my handwriting. But, then, I didn't know for sure.*

He looks down at this list he knows is in his handwriting:

1. Sunday *Times*
2. Lg. Coffee and Danish (me)
3. Lg. Coffee (sugar no milk) and Blueberry Muffin for Cheswick
4. Sm. Decaf (black) and Yogurt (plain) for Cheswick's girlfriend.

Now he remembers that he started out before Cheswick and the others were awake to pick up the items on this list. Halfway there he decided he had the time to take this short walk Cheswick had told him about.

The walk is *glorious,* he thinks, but now he just wants to get back with his *Times* and coffee and settle in. He turns back on the path, headed for town and thinks, *Who knows what all that first list had on it? It could've taken me all day.*

Guild Hall's Markdown in the Age of Mechanical Reproduction

....

O utside the windows, beyond the white deck, where the swimming pool glints deep blue, Rizzoli notices the hand-painted tiles by the pool's edge form an intricate serpentine pattern of turquoise and green. The pool ripples from the unseasonably hot breeze that is coming inside here.

"Rizzoli. Cheswick."

Rizzoli looks up and sees Nicolas motioning for Rizzoli and Cheswick to come over and see the art on the wall, pieces that Nicolas has collected for this, his East Hampton summer place, which he is showing them for the first time this Sunday afternoon.

Rizzoli and Cheswick are old friends and last night at a benefit party they were introduced to Nicolas, who invited them over to see his beach house done in what he calls "severe postmodernist style."

Having arrived here at Nicolas's minutes ago and settled on the couch, the two of them get up now and walk across the parquet floor of the three-story geometric living room, with its towering Spanish windows looking out on the dunes, the sky and the beach.

"Interesting image, but not really a favorite," Nicolas says, pointing to an original, early drip-painting of Jackson Pollock. He pauses. "Paid eight-fifty for it."

$850,000. Sounds like a good purchase price for a Pollock, Rizzoli thinks, but he knows Cheswick feels it's bad form for Nicolas to be so pretentious as to boldly show his art and recite the price he paid for this.

The Hamptonites of Cheswick's crowd are more casually discreet about such things, Rizzoli knows. So, they would say Nicolas was "new money," a term that has always sounded odd to Rizzoli's ears.

"Old money" pretends it has no need for such pretense, and as examples of this type, Rizzoli immediately thinks of Cheswick's family and select others who've summered in style in the Hamptons for decades. *No newer, fancy homes for them.* He thinks of Cheswick's family's summer "cottage," a rambling thirty-room, gray-shingled, old, comfortable place built in the 1920s and he contrasts it with Nicolas's clean, sprawling, white angular 1980s postmodern house combining vastly different architectural styles.

Yet, Nicolas has the finer art collection by far, Rizzoli concludes. *Cheswick has posters while Nicolas has these, originals all, and . . . and this poster.*

"Unusual poster," Rizzoli says, pointing to a framed poster of a Larry Rivers collage with erasures.

"It's a favorite," Nicolas says. He shows them other originals by Johns, de Kooning, Warhol and others but, at the end, Rizzoli decides he loves the Pollock best; he's never seen the image before.

Later, in the afternoon, Rizzoli goes to East Hampton's Guild Hall Museum at Nicolas's suggestion to see the exhibit while

Cheswick and Nicolas shop for dinner. Inside the museum, Rizzoli sees this show is evidently of posters of paintings done by artists who live or have lived in the Hamptons at one time or another—Jackson Pollock, Willem de Kooning, Saul Steinberg, Lee Krasner.

The first poster along the wall of the main gallery that Rizzoli sees is a Saul Steinberg. Next to the framed image of abstracted, colorful beach umbrellas, Rizzoli reads:

From an original by Saul Steinberg
SUMMER STILL LIFE
Reproduction by O'Rooney
4 Color

Rizzoli continues viewing the show. He sees poster after poster of works by these well-known artists. Halfway through the show, near the museum shop, he is curious to see which of these posters they might have for sale.

Inside the shop, Rizzoli notices on the floor a clear Plexiglas container with cardboard tubes *with the posters rolled up inside.*

On the first tube, he reads the label:

Steinberg
SUMMER STILL LIFE

They have the Steinberg. Rizzoli asks the young lady behind the counter if she would mind taking it out of the tube so he can have a look.

"Not at all."

She takes the tube, reaches in, takes out the artwork, opens it out on the counter, holding the opposite edges down so he can get a look.

"It's not a poster," Rizzoli says, surprised.

"No."

No? Rizzoli studies it; he notes:

Signed? "This isn't the original, is it?" Rizzoli asks, incredulously.

"The original," she laughs. "Of course, why else would it be twenty-five dollars?"

"Twenty-five dollars," Rizzoli repeats, trying to be nonchalant. "So, just out of curiosity, the poster of this one in the show, what is the price of it?"

"The poster in the show is museum quality."

Museum quality?

She hands Rizzoli a price list for this show and, leafing through it, he notices the twenty-five-dollar Steinberg original he has before him in that poster version. "One hundred sixty-three thousand?" he asks.

"Sounds right."

Rizzoli hands her back the price list and says, "So, twenty-five for this original?"

"We wouldn't dare ask more," she says, and pointing to a splotch of turquoise in the painting, "You see . . . this awful turquoise, it's blessedly muted by the color separation for the poster printing, . . . and the poster also flattens out this messy painted surface to give the smoothness that appeals to the eye more. O'Rooney, the poster maker, is a master at transforming an original's flaws."

O'Rooney? Rizzoli looks the Steinberg over and says nothing.

"It is signed and dated," she says. "So, for an original, we think it's worth that . . . not so much for the painting itself, . . . but for providing the original inspiration for O'Rooney."

O'Rooney?

Rizzoli is puzzled, yet he doesn't want to seem altogether unknowledgeable, so he risks commenting, "The postcard of this Steinberg original I know is quite valuable, but, how much?"

"Two thousand dollars. Unsigned, of course."

"Two thousand?"

"It is a quite good reproduction . . . nothing remotely near the quality of the museum's poster, of course, . . . but interesting nonetheless for the reproduction technique. It's from O'Rooney's workshop, too, the postcard."

"So many ways to reproduce a painting today, postcards, whatever," Rizzoli says, confused but trying to appear awares.

"Here's a book that's helpful in that regard." She hands a big, dictionary-size book to Rizzoli.

As he begins turning the pages, Rizzoli sees lists. Lists. It lists all the times a single painting has been reproduced since it was originally made, a chronology of each time it was reproduced. And what size and mode each reproduction was:

one inch square, black and white
three by five inches, color
ten feet by fifteen feet, color

And in what medium it appeared, whether:

postage stamp
postcard
billboard
art book
newspaper
magazine advertisement
key chain
T-shirt
bill-cap

Finally, it gives collectors advice on which is the "masterpiece" reproduction of the original.

In the book's introduction, Rizzoli reads a paragraph beginning:

A case can be made for dropping the name of the creator altogether, since, like moviemaking, a painting is now under-

28

stood to be a collaborative process through time. André Malraux once spoke of "a museum without walls" referring to the modern-day mass reproduction of what was known as "fine art." Now people everywhere—printers, magazine editors, art directors, art suppliers, paper merchants, plastics manufacturers, video makers—all join in being "the painter" of a work of art.

Plastics manufacturers?
Rizzoli lets her know he'll take the Steinberg original.
"Any postcards?"
"No, the original will be fine. Thank you."

Rizzoli goes from Guild Hall and meets Nicolas and Cheswick as planned at a new East Hampton bar that Rizzoli has not been to. As they all order drinks, Rizzoli notices hanging from the walls along with Boston ferns are original Pollocks, de Koonings and a Rauschenberg.

While they eat their chips and salsa and drink their beers, Rizzoli casually asks Nicolas if he'd ever consider selling his early Jackson Pollock original.

"For the right price, maybe."
"A thousand?"
"Sure."
"What about the Larry Rivers poster," Cheswick asks, laughing. "Do you want to sell it? It'd fit with my family's other posters."
"Not on my life," Nicolas answers. "Except for that poster, I decorated . . ."
Rizzoli is thinking, *I don't care what anybody thinks . . . I'm thrilled to be the owner of an* ORIGINAL *Pollock . . . and an* ORIGINAL *Steinberg. I might be old-fashioned but . . .*
". . . I decorated my place with original paintings I got at yard sales."
Yard sales?

Nadir to the
Zenith of
City Life

Manhattan

....

A Modest
Proposal for the
City's Homeless

....

"**L**adies and gentlemen, today, on behalf of the great City of New York, I am here to present . . ."

Rizzoli has fallen back into deep sleep for the last hour and now he's dreaming he's at a podium on a stage beginning a speech to a large buzzing crowd. He doesn't know why he is here, or what he is supposed to say. This speech just started flowing out of his mouth this moment:

> . . . to present [pause] His Honor's totally new solution for the problem of the homeless in our great city. *(What? What am I saying? His Honor? Jimmy the Kinder? I can't stand him.)* I repeat: a totally new, innovative solution.

Unable to stop the words coming out of his mouth (*automatically?*), Rizzoli does manage to pause to take in his surroundings a little more. *My speech must be important,* he thinks, noting all the TV cameras and lights up front. And newspaper reporters with tape recorders.

Over there in the front row, nodding and smiling up at him

is a deputy mayor whose face Rizzoli recognizes from the news-
papers. He gives Rizzoli the high sign. *I've joined the administra-
tion? No.* He would leave the stage this instant if he wasn't
riveted to the podium. *I can't run. And I can't stop giving this
speech.*

For those of you here today who may not recognize me, I am
E. P. Rizzoli, the mayor's select urban planning specialist (*It's
true. I'm on the mayor's team!*) for all five boroughs. And I can
tell you, as of today, all the old thinking on the homeless
problem is dead, gone. . . .

The audience is becoming very attentive now and outwardly,
Rizzoli senses that he is coming over very well. But, inwardly,
he panics at thinking, *What solution?* He hasn't the slightest
clue. Yet his lips move and his speech continues:

The mayor, as of this moment, formally announces he is setting aside all prior schemes to deal with the homeless. I know
you were expecting me to announce today, on the mayor's
behalf, the opening of the newest shelter to house the homeless but, no, His Honor has scrapped that along with any
plans to build future shelters in the neighborhoods. . . .

The audience claps. Rizzoli pauses. A note is passed up to
him from the deputy mayor. It reads: "What are you saying?
It's the new shelters you're supposed to be announcing. The
mayor has not authorized your saying more." Rizzoli is startled.
I've gone off the script? What is my script?

His lips move; he senses his hold over the audience—the
sheer power of it. The words come out dramatically. "NO MORE
SHELTERS IN NEW YORK CITY." The applause is deafening.
"And a true, LASTING AND HUMANE, LOW-COST SOLUTION to
the homeless problem." Cheering breaks out as the applause
continues. The deputy mayor is glaring up at Rizzoli, who
averts his gaze.

Waiting for the applause to die down, Rizzoli glances around the room at the banners on the walls: "Humane Solutions for Tomorrow's Quieter, Kinder New York City." Rizzoli knows the mayor recently won reelection on this slogan and Rizzoli suspects this upscale audience here was part of the many taken in by it. Their buttons show it. Rizzoli himself never believed in a quieter or a kinder mayor.

Rizzoli's speech continues:

Mothballed are all these prior timeworn, inadequate responses to the great and humane challenge of providing adequate shelter for the disadvantaged of this richest city on earth. And in their place I present you this quieter, kinder solution. (*Quieter, kinder? I said those words. The slogan? No.*)

There is no need to build more housing of any sort for the homeless. New York City is overbuilt now. Tear down the existing shelters. (*Am I a slick babbler?*) Yes, New York City could house two, three, four, five times the existing homeless with its CURRENT housing stock. I repeat: CURRENT housing stock.

Rizzoli wishes he knew what he was talking about and who, in fact, is talking. *Whose speech is it?* He doesn't know but he continues, with great poise and confidence, saying:

The cost of the quieter, kinder plan I propose? Naturally, you want to know. The cost of the plan is a pittance—and, what's more, there will be a windfall savings from the current shelter program, the costs of which will no longer be necessary. Shelters are not the answer, warehousing people was never the answer. I WILL GIVE YOU THE ANSWER. (*Who's I??*) Listen . . . (*What is it?*)

My proposal would simply offer up all the temporary unused space to the homeless in time-sharing arrangements. While we New Yorkers are away from our homes or businesses.

Rizzoli senses the audience is uneasy about the homeless being dirty or ill and maybe criminals. He doesn't know if his speech has the answer, but it goes on:

> The only homeless eligible for this program would be those without any previous record of crime, drugs or mental illness. (*The speech anticipated this.*) An eligible homeless person would dress, act and speak exactly like yourselves. Why? Because the city would certify him or her through rigorous testing and education in the manners and mores of today's middle-class New Yorker. In short, the city would operate a fine finishing school so all the homeless could come up to middle-class standards with the goal being to make them fit in perfectly to your life-styles. Perfectly . . .

Rizzoli is surprised at where his speech is going; he would never, ever propose such a program himself. *This is not me,* he thinks. But Rizzoli is beginning to like the politics of the program's forcing quieter, kinder New Yorkers and their mayor *to either put up or shut up.* The deputy mayor is scowling at him. His audience is fidgeting. Smiling, Rizzoli goes on:

> And the eligible homeless would be expert in operating the full range of modern appliances—electric toaster, microwave ovens, dishwashers, videorecorders, food blenders, etc. You name it. They would be required to pass rigorous tests on these and hundreds of other appliances.

Rizzoli has none of these items named, but those in the audience seem to have the full range and more of these appliances as they nod approvingly. Rizzoli senses the speech is taking hold of them *despite themselves. Is the speech going to make the program so foolproof, LOGICAL AND HUMANE that they can't possibly turn it down?* He continues:

> Your private bathroom would be a holy shrine for the homeless sharer—he or she would be expertly trained at keeping

your bathroom even more immaculate than you yourself keep it.

With the goal of eventually living in your homes, they would be highly motivated to learn the essentials of behavior that would be acceptable to all of you out there. It would be their one chance. And only after they tested with a proper score in diction, dress, manners, hygiene, etc., would they be able to step into your homes, as proper guests.

Rizzoli knows he almost has them, but he senses his speech *will have to have some guilt-making clincher.* He says the words and listens:

Now, here, who would be hosts? Not most New Yorkers: most are selfish and wouldn't dare share their space—when not used—with a quote middle-class quote homeless person. But there would only be a small percentage of eligible homeless, so, all the plan needs to work is a small number of truly quieter, kinder New Yorkers like yourselves with homes and a willingness to say "Mi casa es tu casa."

The audience breaks into applause.

Statistics give us great hope. Seventy-two percent of all current New York City apartments, condominiums, brownstones, Park Avenue duplexes, East Side town houses—you name it—are deserted each day, every day of the week from nine to five. Now the good news is only 0.0775 percent of that space would need to be shared with the homeless by a few quieter, kinder New Yorkers like yourselves.

Remember, the mayor, in proposing this, wants himself and you to be the ones making possible the quieter, kinder New York for all.

Thank you.

The audience applauds long and loudly; as Rizzoli stands marveling at the way the speech ended, . . . *hanging the mayor on his own petard, as the saying has it.* The deputy mayor glares but he can't do much, with the crowd clapping so approvingly. *Out of guilt.*

"Now I'll take any questions if you have them," Rizzoli says, surprised that he said this. *What?* Just then, the back door opens and Rizzoli sees the mayor himself walk in. *Not the mayor!* The mayor quietly comes around to sit with the deputy mayor and the two talk as Rizzoli answers questions from the audience.

Rizzoli senses the audience has underlying reservations but he erases these, as he ties up ALL loose ends, assuring each of his quieter, kinder questioners variously of the following. Yes, the City will bond the homeless so if anything of yours is broken it will be replaced, free of charge. Yes, the drug-addicted, mentally ill and criminal homeless will have the most humane public treatment possible, but will be prevented from sharing your homes. Yes, the quote middle-class quote homeless will vacate your place by 5:00 P.M., before you arrive home so, essentially, you won't see them. And on and on, even to the point of promising the deposit on bottles would be raised for the homeless to better cover meals. Soap, clean towels and sheets, a basic set of neat, clean clothes, etc., would all be provided free of charge by the City. And on and on.

In answering all, Rizzoli is amazed at what comes out of his mouth; and now, he knows, the speech and the answers afterward have swayed the audience. *And the mayor.* Rizzoli is delighted at having put the mayor on the spot, especially now as he sees the mayor coming up to the podium, having to smile. Rizzoli steps aside, as the mayor says:

Thank you. Thank you, Rizzoli. A quieter, kinder New York City is my dream and it is possible through programs exactly like this one. Just when it seems there's no real solution to the problem of the homeless, there comes along my expert urban affairs specialist, E. P. Rizzoli, and this fine plan.

Now, what I recommend is that a select homeless person be trained and tested by the City of New York and that, starting this coming May 15, Rizzoli himself have the honor of being the first New Yorker to participate in the program by sharing his apartment with this select person for a two-week trial. And judged on the results, I will recommend for or against putting the program into effect. If successful on a trial basis, I promise to put the full program into operation, everywhere in our great city.

Again, our deepest thanks to Rizzoli, and I will eagerly await his report. I personally will share my home with a homeless person, if Rizzoli's report is favorable on June 1, at the end of the trial.

With May 15 three days away on his calendar, Rizzoli is sitting on his red couch alone with the *Times* and unopened mail beside him. Having just read an editorial about himself, he's paused to savor this.

He thinks back to when this all began—that moment the mayor stepped up to the podium. It was exactly then, Rizzoli feels, that he had the quieter, kinder people and their mayor right where he wanted them.

Rizzoli has the *Times* open to the op-ed page. He rereads a quote from the mayor giving credit (*to me*) for devising "this noble experiment in homes for all to be tested for a two-week trial, beginning this Saturday." *"Noble," I like that word.* Rizzoli enjoys the idea of *this mayor being forced to accept . . . a kinder program . . . for once. And the* Times *agrees,* Rizzoli thinks, reading from the editorial, "the Rizzoli Plan for the homeless is a hallmark of a kinder New York City."

Reflecting on the editorial, Rizzoli looks up from the *Times* and realizes how much he does enjoy his recognition as a new political voice with solutions. *I'll have to teach them that mouth-*

*ing "quieter, kinder" political slogans has little to do with the need
to just act as a . . . plain and decent human being.*

Rizzoli vows to be just that, a plan and decent human being,
and to go out of his way to make his homeless sharer feel at
home when he arrives on Saturday. *It's only right I be as polite
as I possibly can.* Rizzoli is concerned to have all work out well
with his homeless sharer, so then *the mayor'll have to take in a
homeless sharer. And the mayor's supporters.*

Rizzoli sets his *Times* down again, picks up his pile of mail,
begins sorting it and finds the letter he's been waiting for. He
opens it and reads who his homeless sharer will be from the
computer printout sent by the City of New York. His name
is Neal Sliboe (pronounced SLY-bow). *That's an unusual name,*
Rizzoli thinks. The printout states he will arrive this coming
Saturday at 9:00 A.M.

Rizzoli finds the printout lacks specifics about Sliboe's background but has a lengthy statistical "profile" on the Sliboe who
has emerged after the City training and retesting. Skimming it,
Rizzoli sees the conclusion has Sliboe's "Middle-Class Home-
Sharer Potential at 70, up 49 points." Averaged into this, Rizzoli
sees his designated sharer's "Proper Politeness at 68, up 57
points" and "Appropriate Dress at 72, up 51 points" and, in-
versely, "Inappropriate Aggression at 14, down 57 points" and
on and on.

Sliboe's dramatic 49 point overall gain, it now strikes Rizzoli,
means his sharer changed himself over completely and that
whoever the base-level Sliboe was, *who began at an average of 21
points . . . now is probably gone . . . forever?* Rizzoli vows to make
all this sacrifice worth his sharer's while.

Scanning other data, Rizzoli reads that the new Sliboe's been
trained to know "34 different household appliances" and on the
list of these appliances, Rizzoli recognizes not a one, except for
his own tiny little vacuum: "Royal Can. Vac. with Dirt Devil
bags." He sees his sharer has also newly mastered the hot-air

popcorn maker and fax machine along with "12 household cleaning procedures." *Twelve?*

After the printout's conclusion, Rizzoli finds a one-page questionnaire filled out in Sliboe's own hand. Birthplace: Unknown. Years without a home: Many. Date of birth: Wish I knew. Rizzoli is touched; his sympathy grows for this man who is trying so hard to be *worthy? of a home.* Rizzoli can't wait to meet him.

The cover letter Rizzoli reads now says that, for orientation, Mr. Sliboe will arrive at 10:00 A.M. the next day "for a personal introduction and any further instructions."

The next day at ten sharp, Mr. Sliboe is at the door. Rizzoli likes him almost immediately. He is reserved and, Rizzoli thinks, *even distinguished-looking, considering he's been out on the streets so long.* A tall man with an angular face, Mr. Sliboe stands a head above Rizzoli as they exchange introductions in the doorway. In his City-issue starched tan chinos, pressed blue plaid shirt and running shoes, Mr. Sliboe seems a little uncomfortable and stands awkwardly with his arm clutching a bundle of clean towels, sheets, a change of clothes, whatever. *Something touching about him.*

"Here, let me take that from you," Rizzoli says, eager to make his new sharer instantly feel at home. Rizzoli puts the bundle in the closet where he's made a special space for Sliboe. He smiles and mentions that to Mr. Sliboe, who then breaks into a smile.

Rizzoli leads him from the entry hallway into the living room, where Mr. Sliboe glances around some and comments about what a nice apartment Rizzoli has.

"Nothing fancy, Mr. Sliboe, but, it's homey."

"I can see that, Mr. Rizzoli. I like that—homey."

"Rizzoli is fine. You don't have to call me 'Mr.'" Rizzoli lets Mr. Sliboe know that he, Rizzoli, is no stickler for other formalities and that Mr. Sliboe should just make himself at home. "My home is your home."

"I know that. Thank you, Mr. Rizzoli."

"Rizzoli. Rizzoli, Mr. Sliboe."

Rizzoli leads Mr. Sliboe over to the dining table by the two windows in the living room and they sit and pass some pleasant conversation. Rizzoli sees more of his sharer: the graying hair parted in middle and neatly brushed, face animated, good laugh. *I like him.* They share some talk about their pasts but Rizzoli doesn't ask how Mr. Sliboe became homeless. *It wouldn't be polite.* Soon, they address the business they have to complete.

Together, they make up a schedule for sharing during the two weeks. Each of the weeks, Monday through Friday, Mr. Sliboe will come in the morning just after Rizzoli has left for work, use Rizzoli's apartment as "home" and sleep on the fold-out red couch, then leave in the evening before Rizzoli comes home from work. That's the way the City wants it, according to instructions Mr. Sliboe delivers.

On Saturdays and Sundays, for the three weekends, Rizzoli learns the City wants them to test sharing on a roommate basis further by being together and getting to know each other better. From 9:00 A.M. to 5:00 P.M. these weekend days, Mr. Sliboe, the instructions say, "will live in the apartment and interface with its prime lessee, namely E. P. Rizzoli." After 5:00 P.M., Mr. Sliboe will leave and go to midtown to sleep in Rizzoli's vacated office, "where a removable, temporary cot and amenities will be provided."

Their schedule started on Saturday, May 15, and now, coming to the end of the trial, Rizzoli thinks, *We're getting along famously.* Today is the final Saturday of the trial. He's up early sitting on his red couch, enjoying coffee before Sliboe arrives. *Famously.*

He would love to tell the mayor of this now but can't because

His Honor demanded of me that no mention whatsoever be made to him of the trial until the full period is up. And no word to the press.

I can't wait to let the mayor know in the report I'll give him in a few days. Gathering some thoughts that will likely go into his report, Rizzoli thinks, *In these past weeks, in every way, Mr. Sliboe has made the transition an easy one. Weekdays, when I come home at 5:30 P.M., he's gone and has left the apartment immaculate . . . much cleaner than I ever kept it . . . always, the couch is made up, dishes washed, trash taken out, everything swept, dusted and tidied up. . . .*

On weekends I enjoy his company. He's adapted to almost all of my routines. He never complains. He even used paper towels in the Melitta when I forgot to buy coffee filters.

On this Saturday, after Sliboe arrives, the two have their usual weekend routines. Rizzoli does the grocery shopping and other of his normal chores. *I can't ask Mr. Sliboe to help. It would be unfair. He's not here twenty-four hours of every day. So, I'll do my usual chores . . . I don't mind . . . it's worth it to me . . . if Mr. Sliboe can stay in and just relish a tiny bit of home. . . . I'll shop for a good dinner.*

Later, Rizzoli has dinner started with a chicken roasting in the oven. He checks it. *It'll be a good dinner,* he thinks as he glances with pleasure at Sliboe enjoying the Saturday afternoon baseball game. *Homeless guy; he deserves these few good meals in God knows how long.*

Mr. Sliboe is very appreciative and polite and, on weekends, does his part in ways that Rizzoli sees. This Saturday, while watching the game, he tidies up the apartment. The bathroom is tidier than Rizzoli has ever seen it *and so clean, it makes me a little uneasy to go in there.*

Still, I'll be accommodating to Mr. Sliboe's neatness. Yet, his apartment is so neat, Rizzoli has a twinge of sadness that he never has the chance to pick up after himself anymore. *And Mr. Sliboe never leaves anything around.*

We have little differences . . . but, nothing major, Rizzoli thinks while putting potatoes in to bake with the chicken. But, the little things can be irritating at times.

Rizzoli is reminded that earlier this afternoon, he discovered his toothbrush in his toothbrush holder, a place where he never keeps it. He tells Mr. Sliboe who smiles and politely reminds him that he, Rizzoli, put it there. *I did?*

I don't remember. Yet, this has happened before. Rizzoli worries, *Are my habits changing? What's with me? A few days will pass and I'll realize I've tolerated something being elsewhere when I've always had it in a certain place . . . like the Ansel Adams photo on the brick wall a week ago. . . . Then when I move the thing back to its original place, Mr. Sliboe reminds me in his polite way that I moved it in the first place . . . and forgot. But, I forget* WHY *I did it in the first place. Am I more absentminded?*

This Saturday evening, after they've had a nice early dinner and Sliboe is gone, Rizzoli is very tired and decides to get in bed. Laying his keys down on the night table, he suddenly hears two voices inside his mind start arguing back and forth.

"Put the keys on the mantel over the fireplace."

"No, the night table."

"FIREPLACE."

"NIGHT TABLE, like always."

Rizzoli has always kept them on the night table. He does resist, but only through tremendous will, and keeps his old way.

The next morning, Sunday, Mr. Sliboe arrives as usual in his friendly polite way. He turns on the day's baseball forecast and begins tidying up the apartment as Rizzoli prepares to go out and do the chores.

Rizzoli exits, but he pauses at the door, thinking, *Did I forget something? What?* He glances back inside his apartment and, to his great surprise, sees himself, Rizzoli, inside there tidying up. *What?* He glances down, he has no body. He realizes he is outside his real body watching someone else moving in his real body there inside the apartment. The one in there slams the door shut. The real Rizzoli is now locked out.

He screams, "Let me in. LET ME IN!" but no sound comes out. He pounds on the door but has no fist. *I'm invisible? . . . a spirit only?* In a rage, he concludes, *Sliboe took my body, forced my spirit out of it and moved his own spirit into my body, lock, stock and barrel. He wanted my apartment and the only way he could get it was to steal my body from me. I can't believe it. HE STOLE MY BODY? AND MY APARTMENT?*

Hours pass as Rizzoli wanders unseen and unheard, through the streets of his old neighborhood, a man without a body. He waits for Sliboe to come out of his, Rizzoli's, apartment. Rizzoli doesn't know what he'll do if he sees *that Slime Sliboe.* Rizzoli's furious at *that Slime Sliboe walking around in . . . my body.* He waits longer but, Sliboe-Rizzoli doesn't appear.

Soon Rizzoli's anger subsides and he starts to blame himself. *Why didn't I see it coming? When I think back on it now I had plenty of forewarnings.* Rizzoli goes over and over the ones he had but ignored.

> *The fights within me to put something back in its old place. And that other voice saying, "No, put it in another place." That was Sliboe inside me fighting to stay. And I'm oblivious.*

> *The day he tells me, "My name's Neal but most people call me Eel for short." Eel? Is that my clue . . . or, what? Him, smiling and saying, "You can call me Eel, if you like." Me, polite in saying, "No, that's okay. I prefer calling you Mr. Sliboe." MR. SLIBOE?*

> *The weekend after that, Sliboe starts calling me "E. P." and I'm still calling him "Mr. Sliboe." "E. P.," he says, "I could use a nice red couch like that when I get my home."*

> *The day he says, "E. P., I want your home" and I laugh thinking, The poor man . . . The Slime.*

• • •

Early morning after his second night outside in the cold, in Central Park, Rizzoli comes across a bench *with Sliboe's discarded old body? It can't be. It is.* It's lying there (*spiritless?*) looking to all appearances as if it is sleeping. It has been there for some while. *Sliboe just threw his body down and came looking for mine.* The clothes on it are dirty, disheveled and rumpled. The shoes are gone. The coat is ripped on the bench.

Rizzoli is desperate; he slips his spirit inside Sliboe's old body and starts off, walking barefoot. Moving Sliboe's tall legs along, Rizzoli, at first, finds it awkward going. The arms are gangly. He notices people staring. But by Columbus Avenue Rizzoli is moving this foreign body along *at a fair clip.*

Turning up Columbus, Rizzoli sees . . . *no. No. It can't be.* Sliboe-Rizzoli is coming this way down Columbus, wearing his, Rizzoli's, brown suit, haircut, red tie, smile, brown shoes, trenchcoat and umbrella.

About twenty paces behind Sliboe-Rizzoli, coming this way too, Rizzoli sees his white-haired friend and longtime landlady, Mrs. Lundy, walking with Louie, who is Rizzoli's bookie from the corner newsstand.

Certain his friends will recognize this Rizzoli impostor, the real Rizzoli starts hollering and pointing, "He's not Rizzoli. I'm Rizzoli. He took my body."

Rizzoli realizes he sounds like the worst of the street babblers. And frightening to other people. His friends.

Sliboe-Rizzoli ignores him and walks past him. Soon Mrs. Lundy passes and frowns at Rizzoli. Louie does the same.

Confused and frightened, Rizzoli quickly moves Sliboe's tattered clothes and gangly body farther up Columbus to stop by a newsstand showing a June 1 *Post.* Reading with Sliboe's weaker eyes, he sees the big headline: RAGS TO RICHES BRONX CRACK KINGPIN: NOT GUILTY. Farther down, in the corner, he comes to a photo of himself, Rizzoli, under the smaller head: Urban

Expert Rizzoli Nixes Own Plan for the Homeless. He reads where Sliboe-Rizzoli reported to the mayor that the two-week trial was "totally unworkable, a waste of time." The mayor is smiling in the photo, next to the impostor Rizzoli.

Only now does Rizzoli realize that *Sly-boo was no homeless person.... He was the mayor's person ... a plant, a fifth column the mayor slipped into my being.* Now that he thinks of it, at work, his boss, the Mayor, had even given hints to him, Rizzoli, and warnings that *I failed to heed. "Remember, hubris blinds worse than acid, Rizzoli." I recall him saying more than once.*

Rizzoli flashes on all the unheeded warnings—Sliboe's and the mayor's—and thinks, *I could kill myself for not catching on. ... MYSELF?*

Rizzoli picks up the *Post,* reads and discovers Sliboe-Rizzoli's solution for the homeless. His solution recommends that all the homeless be rounded up and specially spray painted so they'll instantly become optical illusions. With the spray, the homeless will *appear* to be dressed exactly like the more fortunate many. Homeless men in suits. Homeless women in classy outfits, stockings and heels.

Rizzoli wonders how, garbed in rags but appearing to be otherwise, *we homeless can get any money for food. We'll be dressed too nicely for anyone to give us anything. Anything. At all.* Rizzoli has dummied up now. He knows that's the point.

Public Outrage
at the Sudden
Exposure of
Deeply Private
Matters

·····································

Rizzoli is dreaming when he hears an enormous commotion down in the streets this morning. It wakes him up. He notices he's alone; whoever the woman was in bed with him in the dream is gone. He can't recall the dream. Or what the woman looked like.

Rizzoli moves out of bed toward his window but, in doing so, he notices a note on white paper lying on his desk. He reads:

Dear Rizzoli,
You were even better in bed last night than I ever could've dreamed. In the proper world, we could do this for a lifetime, sweets. For now, just know you're a good piece.

Love,
Stephanie

Stephanie? . . . Stephanie. Sure he knows her and this seems like her edgy humor. *Me? A good piece. But I was alone last night. Was it Stephanie in my dream?* Rizzoli wonders. *But, if so, I could only have dreamed her. . . . Her note here is real, isn't it?* He takes it between his fingers, feels the paper. *I . . . really? slept with* STEPHANIE? . . . *Last night? No.*

Rizzoli has never cared for her; her pretentiousness has always bothered him. *Twenty Bracelets.* It's his own nickname for her. *Beautiful, spoiled. Why has she been interested in me, all this while, when she makes clear to friends she regrets I'm not part of her social world?*

Hell with her . . . Stephanie and her attitudes have always put me off . . . it's why I've avoided her. But, last night, he wonders if he was missing his true love Phoenicia and let his guard down so Stephanie came on to him. *Did she?* He wishes he had a clue.

Gunshots start going off down in the streets. New Yorkers are cursing and shouting everywhere. "NO ONE CAN DO THIS TO ME!" a voice hollers from the street below. "I'LL GET THE ONE WHO DID IT."

Rizzoli hurries to the window and glances out from the top floor. *My God!* Rizzoli sees nothing but pandemonium below. New Yorkers are running helter-skelter, screaming, many brandishing pistols. *Pistols! What is this? First the subway strike. NOW THIS!* Fistfights are going on everywhere. A woman in a dark blue car is trying to jump the curb and run down a fat man fleeing in striped boxer shorts. *Where are the cops?*

WHAT? That's not something burning, is it? Other apartments? Fearing the mob in the street has set fire to buildings, Rizzoli panics and—against his better judgment—throws on his blue jeans, loafers, sweaty T-shirt and blazer, and rushes down the stairs on to 75th.

Rizzoli ducks and runs and darts behind parked cars until he gets to the corner of Columbus Avenue. *Like Sarajevo out here,* he thinks but he is glad for one thing. *No fires, I was wrong there.*

He ducks behind a parked car and finds someone already there, ducking down, a gray-haired guy with lopsided ears but distinguished. Rizzoli asks, "My God, what's going on?"

Motioning for Rizzoli to be quiet and peek around the corner of the car, the guy says in a whisper, "Just watch that shop owner there and then I'll tell you."

"NO ONE IS GONNA SEE THAT. EVER. EVER," the Columbus Avenue shop owner hollers, just as Rizzoli peers around the corner of the car at him. His back is to Rizzoli and he's trying to shield something from view with his whole body. *What is he hiding?* Rizzoli wonders. *He's backing up. Wait, is that a pistol?* The shop owner suddenly shoots out his own shop windows with bursts of automatic fire. A terrible crash rings out as the plate glass shatters on the sidewalk. *Has he gone BONKERS??*

"See there," the guy with Rizzoli says, "he thought the number was embedded inside the plate glass and it wasn't. It's still there."

Rizzoli watches as the shop owner now stands dumbfounded and staring at the same computer green, digital number suspended in midair: $434,608.14. *Number hangs there like a hologram,* Rizzoli thinks. *In pure air.* The shop owner shoots at the number a few more times before helplessly breaking down and weeping. The number hangs there still, undisturbed.

"It is the shop owner's total worth," Rizzoli's companion whispers, "right out there in public. For all of us to see. And look, his finances are even broken down further, for the really interested."

His total worth IS broken down, Rizzoli can see it all now. In smaller digital green letters, below total worth, Rizzoli sees more of this shop owner's private business. His name: Simoli. *Italian, maybe,* Rizzoli thinks. His shop's name: Ricci & Ricci Wear. *Never been inside.* There follows a summary breakdown of his other assets: two houses, three cars, stocks, bonds, mutual funds, IRAs. *The works,* Rizzoli concludes. *The works.*

"He's no different," Rizzoli's companion says. "See, all the shop owners' assets are right there at eye level, all up and down Columbus. Just happened this morning instantly. Bam, it was suddenly all out there, BAM!"

"Glad I'm not a shop owner," Rizzoli says. His companion nods and says, "Me, too." Rizzoli can't help glancing over at Louie's newsstand: "$54,212.08." *Louie?* Rizzoli is astounded that Louie is worth so much. *Louie?* The Japanese restaurant, with his favorite Domburi, has only "$7,804.76." *No. He's always busy. What's he doing with his money?*

"TRY AND HIDE YOUR WORTH FROM ME NOW, SIMOLI!" a voice suddenly shouts. Rizzoli looks and sees what must be some creditor of Simoli who has just arrived on the scene. "Four hundred thousand big ones you owe me! And yesterday before I knew this, you poor-mouthed me for another loan. THIS is the LIMIT, even if I am your father-in-law. HERE, LET ME PAY YOU BACK." He fires a pistol and Simoli falls.

He killed Simoli, Rizzoli thinks terrified.

"NOW, TRY AND HIDE YOUR SECOND HOUSE FROM ME, SI-MOLI!" the enraged pistol-wielding man screams at the bleeding corpse.

Rizzoli is terrified at this turn of events. He crawls under a parked car. He doesn't know what happened to his companion. He lies there waiting and listening. A bright sun comes out, as he hears more angry voices on Columbus.

"WAIT UNTIL MY LAWYER HEARS ABOUT YOUR HIDDEN ASSETS," some woman screams, at the same time as some guy's hoarse voice shouts, "So, all that time you were secretly piling up all this money, not saying a word. I hope you're proud of yourself, SLIME!"

Is he gonna die? Rizzoli asks. *Is this one dead, too?*

"SLIME."

Shots ring out again. Feet run away. All is suddenly quiet as Rizzoli waits; then, suddenly, he overhears Louie from the newsstand saying to someone. "It's true. People *don't* realize what a fortune you can make operating a Lotto machine. The fifty or sixty Lotto newsstands that I have a piece of gross . . . GROSS . . . millions annually. . . ."

Louie? A real millionaire.

After a long lull, Rizzoli peers out cautiously from under the car. *No dead bodies.* He looks around. *No Louie.* He sees a guy walking on the other side of the street. *What's that over his head? It's not. IT IS.* "$412.37" appears plain as day over his head. *He must not know it is there.* Rizzoli thinks. *Now it's not just shop-keepers. It's EVERYBODY?*

Rizzoli sees others walking in the bright sunlight with numbers over their heads. He thinks, *Maybe the sunlight brought out their numbers. Like a flame bringing out secret writing in lemon juice.* Rizzoli has a nightmare image of a future subway ride with everyone sitting across from one another, silently, all with their total assets above their heads.

Rizzoli crawls out from under the car and joins the bewildered crowd streaming along the sidewalk, with everyone having a green, digital number over his head.

A "$208.00" woman suddenly turns to a "$323.16" man and says, "To think I thought you had money!"

At the curb, Rizzoli sees a white stretch limousine parked with its chauffeur behind the wheel showing personal assets of thirty thousand something.

Up ahead, on the sidewalk, Rizzoli notices a man running with "$504,347.71" in total assets including "Cocaine: $354,789; Wrist watch: $10,678; Pair of shoes: $2,367." *Poor bastard has nowhere to hide,* Rizzoli thinks. *NOWHERE.*

"STOP IN THE NAME OF THE LAW!" a voice shouts across the street and Rizzoli looks over there to see a gun-wielding "$734.86" policeman chasing a "$12,856.00" suspect who is running. Rizzoli recognizes the suspect as the father-in-law who lent money to Simoli, *who was worth four hundred thousand something.* The cop shoots and the suspect crumples to the pavement. *Simoli's father-in-law dead? What next?*

Just then, Rizzoli's attention is diverted to a short arrogant man swaggering toward him on the sidewalk, obviously proud that his total worth can now be exhibited to the world. He wears a white suit and a panama hat and carries a white cane. The green figures over his head are flashing. *Has to be his stocks plunging. What else?* The unsuspecting gentleman keeps smiling and swaggering and throwing his head back. *Guy wants everybody to know his worth!* Rizzoli can barely keep from bursting into laughter as the guy gets into the backseat of the white stretch limo with its chauffeur now worth more than the gentleman himself. A passerby shouts the truth at the limo's dark opaque back window.

Rizzoli passes a beggar with "$23,412.00" over his head and a guy shouting at him, "YOU MEAN I GAVE YOU QUARTERS FOR YEARS AND YOU BANKED THEM? YOU'RE WORTH MORE THAN I AM! GIVE ME BACK MY QUARTERS!"

"Hey, Rizzoli?" someone suddenly shouts. *It's Cheswick,* Rizzoli thinks and turns around to see his friend striding up.

"I had no idea. What's this? You're worth that?" Cheswick asks. Suddenly Rizzoli realizes he too must have a figure over his head. He looks but he can't see it because it's over his head.

"With that kind of money, you borrow my white shirt?" Cheswick asks. "Don't let Stephanie see your new worth or she'll be after more than just getting into your pants."

"Hey, Cheswick," Rizzoli says, shrugging. "Cheswick."

"Don't Cheswick me," Cheswick says, "maybe along with buying yourself more dress shirts, you can manage to pay me the money I won from you in the football pool last fall, or, can't you afford it?" Cheswick storms off down Columbus.

"Hey, what does the figure over my head say?" Rizzoli asks the first person coming down the street, a black kid in a red running suit.

"$614,512 and some change. You one rich sucker, bro," the kid says. "And here on your back it say you got three houuuses and I ain't got one, dude."

Six hundred thousand something, did the kid say? But I know I *only have $1,700 total in the bank. THIS OTHER BREAKDOWN, DID HE SAY? THREE HOUSES? Can't be, I'm lucky to have the rent on the apartment covered for this month. WHOM DO YOU GO TO? TO COMPLAIN?*

Rizzoli decides someone at the Chemical Bank ought to know so he starts off for his local branch, at Columbus and 72nd. Nearing it, he notices inside there are no people and it's darkened. *What?* he wonders as he tries the door and finds it locked. On the inside, he sees this notice and reads:

Dear Customer,
Chemical Bank is closed today, June 18, and will remain so for an indefinite period. The Federal Banking Regulatory Commission has ordered Chemical Bank and all other banks in the New York City area to close pending an investigation into the recent, sudden phenomenon of widespread public exposure of private financial affairs.
THANK YOU FOR BANKING AT CHEMICAL.

Chemical is closed indefinitely? What does this mean? Rizzoli wonders. He moves to the automatic teller to get his checking account balance. The slip comes out and it reads $1,714.18. *My total assets. That's what I thought. It hasn't changed,* Rizzoli thinks. *How could it?*

Rizzoli is hopeful now that the financial figure showing above his head maybe has come into line with his seventeen-hundred-dollar worth. He asks a passerby, "Would you check my worth?"

"You got seven hundred ninety-three thousand somethin'," the stranger informs Rizzoli.

That's more than it said earlier. I only have checking. No stocks, no bonds, nothing else. And I'm going UP? What is this? Rizzoli thanks the person and heads up Columbus. *The mistake is getting BIGGER?*

On the sidewalk, moving along, Rizzoli quickly passes the

expensive boutiques, the exotic restaurants, the bars, the expensive shoe stores, the ice cream parlors—all with their finances newly bared to public view. Rizzoli scans some of the places' finances as he walks: for Priscilla Lingerie, "Yearly income: $132,691; Assets: $79,564; Liabilities: $1,267,489," and for Sterling & Atkins Apparel, about the same in income and assets but only $1,103,345 in Liabilities. It's generally the same financial picture all along.

I'm going up. They're in the hole, Rizzoli asks, *Is it all a* BUBBLE? *APPEARANCE? No, can't be. But, wait . . .*

In the far distance, on the opposite sidewalk coming this way, he sees Stephanie, as beautiful as ever, dressed stylishly. He doesn't want to have to talk to her. He ducks down behind a parked car out of the way.

"Yo, dude."

Rizzoli hears the black kid. He turns around.

"Wait now, you be richer than before. You past eight hundred grand now. And you still streakin'."

Still streaking! No! No! The mistake is BALLOONING? Rizzoli is beside himself. *No!*

"You be nine hundred now," the kid exclaims. "And you still movin' on out."

A crowd gathers, stopping to watch now as the cool green figures on Rizzoli's back add nearer and nearer to the magical million mark. They stare at Rizzoli, who fears Stephanie might come over, see how inflated his worth is and really get interested in him.

He is embarrassed that his worth is so hugely inflated and getting worse by the minute. *Who am I fooling?* He meets the crowd's gaze, feeling sheepish, smiling.

The crowd becomes animated now. Small children squeal as Rizzoli's worth balloons. A "$2,412.00" lady holds her breath and smiles at Rizzoli. Many hold their breath and move their lips counting as the numbers behind Rizzoli's head go higher and higher. An "$804.00" burly guy comments that Rizzoli "is a flesh an' blood Lotto jackpot with more and more money."

"ALL RIGHT! HE DO IT!" the black kid shouts. "ALL RIGHT, BRO, YOU BE A MILLIONAIRE." The crowd erupts into applause and clapping.

Rizzoli feels ashamed; he wishes he could hide his new digital worth. *This is what Simoli must have felt like,* Rizzoli thinks. He feels uncomfortable and confused.

Rizzoli is wondering what he has to do next when suddenly the back door swings open on the white stretch limousine with the smoked windows, which has remained parked at the curb all this while. The limousine's owner gets out of the backseat and Rizzoli recognizes the man in the white suit whose fortune was declining earlier on the sidewalk. It's still declining and Rizzoli can see it's down to the point where the gentleman has less than half his chauffeur's worth. Seemingly aware that his worth is flashing a steady decline, the gentleman asks if Rizzoli would be interested in the limousine for half price. "I'll take thirty thousand dollars for it. It's not even a year old," he adds, "and I'll throw in the remaining three months on the chauffeur's contract."

A limo? Rizzoli thinks. *Never.* Through the years there is nothing Rizzoli has ever loathed more than seeing this same white stretch limo parked here on Columbus taking up two parking places. *NEVER.*

"I'll give you twenty thousand. Take it or leave it. I'll write you a check right here," says Rizzoli. His very words flabbergast him. *WHAT AM I SAYING? I KNOW I HAVE $1,700 TOTAL. I CAN'T BUY A LIMO.* "Take it or leave it," Rizzoli repeats.

The gentleman's worth has visibly declined in the few minutes he has been negotiating and he reluctantly agrees, saying, "Fine. Fine."

No. No. I can't do this, Rizzoli tells himself even as he opens his blazer and gets out his wallet with his Chem Bank checkbook, which was the only thing he remembered to take when he had thought his apartment was burning. He writes out the $20,000 check, with his mind screaming at him, *No! No! Yours IS A RUBBER CHECK AND YOU DESPISE LIMOS, YOU PHONY.*

Rizzoli can't seem to help himself; his body's sudden impulse to buy overwhelms what his mind tells him. He hands over the check and gets into the backseat of the limo. The crowd cheers. He waves.

You PHONY, his mind screams at him.

He waves again. In the plush backseat, he sits waving, with the digital numbers flashing a cool green million over his head and his mind screaming at him, *PHONY, PHONY.*

Rizzoli closes the door. The "$804.00" burly guy from the crowd sticks his face up close to the smoked window and says to the unseen Rizzoli, "Your becoming a millionaire, pal, has renewed my faith in the American Dream."

THE AMERICAN DREAM IS A $20,000 LIMO PAID FOR WITH A $1,700 BANK ACCOUNT?

WAKE UP, his mind shouts to him, *before your American Dream becomes a NIGHTMARE.*

Rizzoli knows his mind is talking common sense. *But MY BODY'S IMPULSE WON'T OBEY IT.*

Suddenly, his arm is being clasped and there getting in the other door to sit next to him in the backseat is Stephanie, who says, "Oh, Rizzoli, why didn't you tell me?" She kisses him.

"I wanted you to find out for yourself," Rizzoli answers with a smile. *YOU PHONY! YOU DON'T EVEN CARE FOR HER.*

She whispers in his ear that she has on the same "black string bikini panties" she did "last night."

String . . . panties? Last night is more than a dream?

As the limousine pulls away, Rizzoli knows the crowd thinks he, Rizzoli, has just made it big, in jeans still and driving away in a limousine, worth a million with a beautiful, stylish woman on his arm. He can see it in their eyes.

But only Rizzoli knows the true dilemma of his mind wanting him to be his old, true self while his body has him keeping up appearances. *This is a nightmare,* Rizzoli thinks, SOMEBODY MUST HAVE SET ME UP AS THIS PHONY PUBLIC MILLIONAIRE. BUT, WHO SET ME UP?

He stops himself; he's suddenly stunned to think of himself for the first time as *a millionaire. Rizzoli the Millionaire.*

Summering
in Style

Money-Changing
Matters Among
the Right
Hamptonites

....

H ere, as the guest of honor, sitting opposite the head of the table at this large, very social Hamptons summer dinner party, Rizzoli is glancing at the other guests—diplomats, socialites, fashion and film sophisticates—when he is suddenly aware that he's eating his fish off this elegant Limoges china plate with his spoon. *What the . . . ?*

Down the table, a supermodel glances up at him (her face he instantly recognizes, *but what is her name?*), takes a cue and so puts down her fork, then her fish knife and picks up her spoon to use to eat her fish.

Rizzoli sees her and debates switching to his fork and fish knife like the other guests. Knowing this will confuse the model, he hesitates but thinks he should switch to the proper utensils anyway. Waiting until he thinks no one will notice, he goes to set down his spoon and pick up the fish fork, all the while reminding himself to hold it properly.

He tries, but he can't switch. *No.* He keeps on eating his fish with his spoon. He struggles silently, still without success.

When he looks up, all the guests are eating their fish with their spoons.

This surprises Rizzoli but, he thinks, *since I'm the special guest, no one wants to correct me probably.*

Being nonchalant about this is my best bet, Rizzoli thinks, raising a piece of chili-crusted salmon to his mouth on his spoon while casually glancing down the long table at the many distinguished guests at this lavish East End party. *They all seem to be here. In my honor?*

Why exactly are they here? Rizzoli doesn't know. But, he knows that the host and hostess, Harold and Illiana, who are both at the far end of the table, are legendary Hamptons party givers.

Rizzoli catches them looking his way, smiling and he smiles back. Then, they smile at the young woman sitting to his right and Rizzoli turns and sees it's their daughter, Stephanie, whom he has known for some years. She squeezes his arm.

Stephanie's warmth and her being by his side here at dinner with her famous parents and their friends is unusual to Rizzoli. *In the past, her interest in me was purely physical.*

Tonight, her parents and all their wealthy friends seem to be honoring the two of them. *Why?* He doesn't know. Rizzoli is just glad he has good table manners. *Or, used to . . . before tonight.*

Stephanie is a beauty and, with tanned face, dark eyes and long black hair, she is turned to admire him when somebody down the table says, "Oh, look at the colors. The sun has just set over the ocean. How beautiful!"

The guests stop conversing for the moment and, like Rizzoli, glance out the cathedral-ceiling windows, at the lawn, slipping down past the aqua pool to the beach and the rosy Atlantic. The beach is golden and Rizzoli thinks, *The entire Hamptons must now be bathed in this golden light. All its summer people aglow in it.*

Averting his gaze from the scene out there, Rizzoli sees himself in his fine white double-breasted suit reflected in a window, but now, with a shadow falling on its surface, the window reveals something about him that was not there moments ago—green digital numbers flashing over his head.

My total worth's still flashing over my head, . . . first showed there a few days ago . . . and appeared to make me rich. Do the numbers still make him appear that rich; he wonders, but he doesn't know since the green figures are reversed in the reflection.

I'm the only one showing worth. This Hamptons crowd have no green numbers over their heads. What does it mean?

My worth a few days ago was greatly exaggerated, one million dollars . . . when $1,714 was what I had in the bank. Can't be different now, can it?

"How much am I worth?" Rizzoli hears himself say. *Out of nowhere.* All heads turn toward Rizzoli. They stop conversation. He can't believe he asked this.

How gauche. Rizzoli also thinks his question might well bring the answer "$1,714." *The truth but an embarrassingly modest sum for this crowd.* He can only smile.

"Total, $883 million," the elegant gray-haired lady next to him declares, smiling pleasantly.

A more preposterous sum than even a few days ago, Rizzoli thinks, and instantly vows not to go on with this charade. *I'm going to tell them all. Now. Right here. Tell them, "The figures are wrong. My real worth is . . ."*

He tries. He can't. This makes him think he has to be *a captive of appearance . . . and the power I think it gives me.*

"Thank you," Rizzoli says, still smiling. "Thank you. You probably think I'm another narcissistic multimillionaire."

"No," says some guest.

"Noooh," echoes another.

"No. It's understandable you're curious," Stephanie says, smiling at him radiantly, her dark eyes looking hypnotically at

Rizzoli. He sees her lovely graceful body, all deep tan in the gauzy black off-the-shoulder dress. "You just want to know . . . What do we see in you."

"A rich and powerful young man," a voice offers from down the table.

"Yes."

"Yes."

Smiles show. Silverware starts clinking. As the conversation begins again, Rizzoli smiles into Stephanie's beautiful face.

Looking deep into her eyes, he recalls Stephanie telling him earlier before dinner about how her father had checked out Rizzoli's credentials. "My accounting firm tells me the stock and bond quotations over his head are up to the minute," he had told his daughter and then *Stephanie passed on to me how impressed her father was with that.*

Suddenly, it's clearer to Rizzoli that the interest Stephanie and her famous father and his friends are showing in him *is because of my . . . "appearance" of great worth.*

So how long will I be putting them on? he asks himself. *How long?* He wishes he knew and whether he can stop himself.

Suddenly, the conversation at the table politely shifts and the older, stylish woman on Rizzoli's left turns to him and begins speaking charmingly of how she had always had this dream of designing a line of dresses for $500,000 or more apiece.

Rizzoli smiles, asks questions about her projected line of luxurious dresses, all the while making charming conversation, when suddenly he gestures and knocks over her glass, sending water spilling onto her lap.

Rizzoli grabs his napkin and starts dabbing (*Her crotch! No!*) as she keeps smiling and talking demurely. He hopes no one else is paying attention as he, Rizzoli, goes on wiping up her crotch; he can't keep himself from doing it and is aghast he didn't just apologize and offer her his napkin. *That would have been the proper thing to do.*

Why can't I do the proper things? he wonders, frantic. *Is it that I'm "nouveau"* . . . *and my sudden wealth forces me to have these bad manners, or what?*

The lady, a genuine ageless beauty, now asks him breathlessly, "Are you looking to invest in any worthy projects like my dresses, Mr. Rizzoli?"

He smiles back at her, as he finishes blotting her lap dry with his napkin, leaving a dark circle. "Excuse me," he interrupts the table conversations. "How much am I worth now?" *No.* He cringes for himself. *Am I gauche or what?*

"Total, $920 million," comes the answer from down the table. "Maybe a billion by the end of this evening."

"I don't know why I'm so curious anymore. It just keeps on going up. . . . And that's no surprise."

Pleasant laughter breaks out all around the table as Rizzoli feels like disassociating himself from himself. He can't, even though he wants to.

A dark-haired young male actor next to the gray-haired woman addresses Rizzoli with a stroking I've-never-seen-any-body-so-visibly-rich-as-you conversation about a movie project he's always wanted to get off the ground.

Stephanie overhears, turns and whispers, "Speaking of future movies, Rizzoli's promised he's going to see my father's project through, haven't you, Rizzoli?"

Promised? With what?

Rizzoli nods agreement coolly. Now, he's clear; with her producer father viewing him as a big investor, Rizzoli realizes all the Hamptonites here tonight must see him as the potential angel who could make their projects come true, too.

While they finish their main course, Rizzoli can see the occasional guest trying to be nonchalant and steal a look at the top of Rizzoli's head. *A billion. I'm moving toward becoming a billionaire. The figures, I mean, are moving toward it. Not me.*

Rizzoli smiles at Stephanie, says, "My investment in your father is good as gold." Then, turning to converse with the actor, he reaches with his spoon in front of the elegant woman and takes the last piece of salmon off the actor's plate. The actor smiles. Rizzoli eats it. Then he reaches and picks at the actor's plate, finally helping himself to the last carrot.

He looks up. Those guests who have finished begin eating off the plates of guests who still have food.

The guests smile, following his example, he knows, because *they all want to avoid causing embarrassment to themselves by not sharing in my ways . . . especially since they see I'm growing richer by the minute. They want to make a good appearance with me by showing bad manners.*

At this, Rizzoli suddenly realizes, with his worth expanding so impressively, in time, *I could transform all good manners into bad. And bad to good. Couldn't I?*

Rizzoli realizes he's just had a power fantasy *of a true nouveau riche sort,* and this shocks him *down to my . . . core. CORE?*

Movie Project
in Development
at the American
Hotel at 2 A.M.

....

A beautiful woman alone at that table in the corner, Rizzoli thinks, as he glances around the back dining room at the American Hotel. *Another single woman at that other table, too. Intellectual-looking woman.*

Harold and I and the two women are the only persons still having dinner this late tonight. Fans in this back room, hot night. What time is it anyway? No clock.

Rizzoli has grown tired here during dinner from listening to Harold present *yet another of these endless Hamptons development deals. Everything is development projects here in the Hamptons in summer, each one needing investors to complete. Nothing finished.*

Empty tables wait with white tablecloths, starched napkins and wicker chairs as Rizzoli glances around the vacant end of the room, then at the wall with its nineteenth-century prints against patterned rose wallpaper.

"Rizzoli," Harold, the well-known Oscar-winning movie producer, says, against the soft strains of Gershwin coming from the baby grand in the other dining room, "so, let me give you more details about this development deal of mine." Harold stops speaking; his mouth is full.

Rizzoli waits politely and, while using his fish knife deftly on his grilled swordfish, he studies the famous producer. He sees a stylish older man with classical features setting off his short-cropped Roman-like hair. Harold is in casually elegant summer attire: a coral-colored linen jacket, white pants and pastel tie.

"Rizzoli," Harold says in his deep voice, "in the movie business, to continue being successful, I've had to keep setting trends, taking the giant leap ahead. This project is in that vein exactly—so exciting, it is going to reshape movie viewing for years to come. What's more . . ."

Rizzoli isn't listening; he's glanced down to see what he himself is wearing. He's surprised, *It's my style at least.* A Matisse tie with a light olive double-breasted sport coat. Light blue shirt.

Confident about his dress and eating well with his fish knife, Rizzoli is relieved to think, *Maybe I've become more of a gentleman and less nouveau riche than I was a few weeks ago, when I became an instant multimillionaire and came out to the Hamptons.*

". . . So, I want you to have the chance to get in on the deal early," Harold is saying, "after all you might wind up being my son-in-law so, it'd be in the family."

Rizzoli is still not paying attention. Instead, he is looking across to the far garden-court dining room at a big mirror with his and Harold's reflections. *And the intellectual woman's.*

Over his own head's reflection, Rizzoli sees the green digital numbers flashing his worth, instant to instant, in mirror image. Rizzoli reads it backward. *$720 million and something is my total worth—a drop from a week ago but rising again.*

"So, tell me more," Rizzoli says, trying to be polite.

As Harold continues talking about his movie deal, what Rizzoli really notices is Harold's stroking you-are-so-key-to-this-project tone of voice. Rizzoli is amused that *ever since I've had these fake millions hanging over my head, people like Harold play to me . . . see me as key, these important Hamptons types.*

Rizzoli never used to be treated like this by these people. *Now, I've come to expect it. It's changing me.*

Truth is . . . Rizzoli can't fool himself. He's still worth only $1,714. He knows that for a fact. *I've known that all along.*

Why fool Harold? Why not try telling him the truth? Rizzoli can't. He knows why. *I'm still in the grip of appearances.*

What's more . . . Rizzoli has a vague memory *(from somewhere)* of when he tried to tell people the truth, they just laughed and chose, instead, to believe what their eyes told them.

"Harold, so you were saying about your project in development," Rizzoli repeats. "Sorry, my mind wandered for an instant there."

Harold looks miffed for a split second but smiles and says, "Yes, as I was explaining, you're aware I'm sure that my last film project grossed $110 million but you don't know the real budget . . ."

REAL?

". . . real budget for that film was only $40 million, NOT . . ."

It was padded.

". . . NOT the $60 million that was reported in the trades. So, you figure it—more insider's profit.

"This movie is supposed, SUPPOSED . . . to cost $80 million. REAL BUDGET? Forty-five. Fifty mil.

"YET, it will also earn more. Why, Rizzoli? It's true to life. So true, the moviemaking will be reinvented . . . in the process . . ."

Moviemaking . . . REINVENTED?

". . . so, as an independent producer, I need a guy with deep pockets, willing to dare, a guy precisely like you, Rizzoli. What do you say?"

"What I'm willing to do is this," Rizzoli answers, startling himself by beginning to propose something he doesn't know what, "when I decide to leave our dinner this evening, I'll invest

69

my gain, provided my worth has registered a gain for this evening."

Harold smiles agreeably.

"My base worth was $718 million—that was what it registered when we walked in here to have dinner. So, what am I worth now, Harold?"

Harold glances up over Rizzoli's head. "$720 million."

"Up two million," Rizzoli adds, suddenly having the insight about why he's proposed this—he wants to get this dinner over but not seem impolite to the famous producer.

"So, Harold, what do you say we call it an evening?"

Rizzoli can see Harold looks disappointed. *Listen to him a little while longer,* Rizzoli urges himself. *That way he'll be happy, yet my worth won't go up a lot more. Two million is about what I'm comfortable investing, at any rate.*

"We'll keep talking a little while more, Harold, if you like, just remember, I can't guarantee my numbers won't disappear into thin air, and if so, you lose. But, with this two-million-dollar gain, I'll write you a check here and now." *WHAT? Your millions are all the bank's computer error, you know that. You don't have that kind of money. You're acting the role of Big Shot, . . . playing the market.*

"If you don't mind, I'd like to keep talking," Harold says, grateful at the offer to speculate in Rizzoli a little more.

"So, what about the script?" Rizzoli asks boldly, hoping to direct the conversation and not have Harold ramble on endlessly about his development project. "Tell me."

Harold explains the current scriptwriter is "fantastic. Name is Theresa. She's a high-key, nervous sort. Rewrites a lot. Sees everything as a movie. Incredible.

"The script is being finished. Theresa has it all up to this point. It's more real than a movie, I tell you. Here, take a look at this," Harold says, reaching into his fine leather slipcase and pulling out a script. "Take a glance. It's the script to date."

Rizzoli puts on his glasses and glances at the front page. It reads:

WHICH IS IT? NIGHT? OR DAY?
An original screenplay by Theresa Ulman

HIGH ANGLE SHOT OF MAGICIAN
He strides with authority, laughing, on modern-day Main Street, with the village's nineteenth-century, three-story brick building, a hotel, in the foreground.

CAMERA LOWERS. CAMERA ZOOMS IN
BEGIN TITLES OVER busy summery Main Street with passersby.

CLOSE SHOT — MAGICIAN

MAGICIAN
This moment is the highlight of all the time before and after, if you know this right moment before it's past.

What? Rizzoli flips to the last page of the script as Harold says, "The dialogue there is fresh, honest." Rizzoli reads the last lines of dialogue:

THE PRODUCER
The dialogue there is fresh, honest.

THE INVESTOR
Yes.

Rizzoli looks up and says, "Yes," then reads:

THE PRODUCER
What's in the script there really plays, as we say in the business.

Rizzoli looks up, as Harold looks his way and says, "What's in the script there really plays" — Harold moves his fingers to make quotes around the word — "as we say in the business."

"Uh-huh," Rizzoli says, reading "THE INVESTOR: Uh-huh."

"In fact," Harold says, "the scriptwriter Theresa, happens to be the woman sitting over there at the other table now."

Rizzoli glances up in the mirror and sees Harold's indicated she's the intellectual-looking woman. Rizzoli focuses on the reflection of this scriptwriter, who is unaware she is being observed. So Rizzoli studies her intense expression. He can almost sense her mind working.

"Right now she's working out what's next, seeing a scene, hearing dialogue. You can bet on it," says Harold. "If she wasn't working, I'd introduce you."

What Harold said just then . . . is not dialogue in her mind, is it? Harold and I are not in her mind, voices making up dialogue for this scene she wants. We're not specters she fantasizes in a scene not yet written, are we?, Rizzoli wonders, before he asks, "The female lead. You have a star in mind?"

"Right over there," Harold motions with his head in back of him.

Looking to secure his possible investment, Rizzoli glances over at the beautiful woman and sees she has no panties on.

"Gabriella's her name. She's breathtaking," Harold says. "Men are riveted by her."

"She is a beauty," Rizzoli notes, while the exposed untanned V where her tanned legs come together under her short skirt holds his gaze steady.

Its focus draws his gaze nearer and nearer until he experiences himself transformed into a camera view zooming in closer and closer to her crotch.

Leaving out his body and everything else from the surroundings, his view comes closer and its frame narrows until he is seeing only her full curved thighs, crotch, stomach. Her head and feet are outside his view.

Can she see me moved in this close, staring up her crotch? He hopes not; he hopes it's like the movies when the person in close-up doesn't know the camera is doing it.

Coming in closer still, he stops suddenly, inches away, looking up her dress. *Am I in a freeze-frame? Where's my body?* he asks as his gaze just hangs suspended there. Seeing her crotch in telephoto view, Rizzoli feels his own body is this close to her, too.

He senses she'll scream any second. He's terrified she'll do so, and then his gaze pans back to where he was sitting at the table. He can't see himself, but his swordfish leftovers are still in front of him on the plate.

Rizzoli gazes up. Harold is a giant head, as tall as a man, filling up most of the dining room.

A close-up of Harold. His face, is it? The features are looming so large, Rizzoli can't tell. *And Harold's ear is not showing.* CROPPED? *Cropped out, is it?*

AM I OUTSIDE THE FRAME? *Where am I?*

Rizzoli glances up at the mirror to see if his own reflection is still there to orient himself. He sees the same wall mirror from before coming closer, growing larger until it frames out all of the room, showing only the image of the changing digital numbers, showing now $1.2 billion. $1.25 billion.

The mirror reflects no other images, no reflection of him, Rizzoli, only numbers flashing so high, Rizzoli doesn't know anymore if they're his numbers.

Cutting away from the mirror, Rizzoli suddenly feels himself to be a giant head. *IN THE FRAME.* His lips move, like two giant sea bass, as he says, "Harold, I feel we're alive in her mind only. We're in the scene she's imagining, we're close-ups right now."

"Don't be silly," Harold says, his giant white teeth showing two feet long, top and bottom. "If I'm a close-up, I'd know it, believe me."

Silly? Rizzoli is frightened that Harold is blind to what's happened and the terror is all his, Rizzoli's, to see.

73

He calms himself by telling himself he's really experiencing nothing unusual and, in fact, he's just back finishing dinner with Harold and *the close-up mirror is imaginary, the figures pure fantasy. Nothing real.*

Rizzoli closes his eyes and takes comfort in recalling the solid feeling he had just moments ago, *When I was at a steady $720 million.* He wishes his worth were down there again, instead of going up so high he can't relate. He wishes it'd be back at 720.

Rizzoli still has his eyes closed but feels his giant fish lips wanting to say, "Harold. I've got to go now. So, what's the gain?"

He opens his eyes. The mirror says $1.8 billion. Huge-faced Harold is talking on.

Harold's scriptwriter has Harold . . . taking millions in . . . in talk. She's not giving me the line, "I've got to go, Harold."

What's behind all this? Rizzoli wonders and a deep voice (OFF-SCREEN? A NARRATOR?) answers, "Behind all this . . . is NOTH-ING. The VOID."

Back to
Everyday
City Life

Manhattan
....

Urban Rage
with Monday
Alternate Sides
of the Mind
Perceiving

....

Rizzoli dreams it's a hot, already humid Monday morning nearing eleven o'clock as he and his landlady, Mrs. Lundy, sit inside Rizzoli's Rabbit with the engine running, while parked on the uptown side of their block on West 75th, just in from Central Park West.

As Rizzoli warms up the Rabbit, Mrs. Lundy takes up the conversation at the point where she had left off talking with him minutes ago in her apartment. "So like I was telling you, Rizzoli," Mrs. Lundy begins, "I always know what my ex-husband is thinking before he even knows. His problem is that he underestimates me. When I turn the . . ."

Rizzoli is only half listening. He sees most of the cars have already been moved from this side of the street and are now on the other side, temporarily double-parked in a row alongside the row of cars that don't have to move today by eleven o'clock.

". . . turn the tables on him you should see his face," Mrs. Lundy continues. "Last night you should have seen his face."

Rizzoli listens and knows that Mrs. Lundy is upset, but won't admit it. Earlier, when he came to her apartment, she had informed him that the night before her ex-husband, Mr. Lundy, with whom she claims to be on friendly terms, had made one of his infrequent visits.

Now, before leaving this good parking place, Rizzoli, out of habit, double-checks the official street sign. He reads: "Tow-Away Zone. NO PARKING 11 AM–2 PM Mon. Wed. Fri. Dept. of Traffic." Today *is* Monday and, seeing "Mon.," Rizzoli is satisfied he has no choice but to move. He always checks.

Having read the sign, Rizzoli gets his usual, instant twinge of hatred for the message and the rigmarole of the street sweepers, meter maids, cops and City Hall. *And the street sweeper never comes,* Rizzoli thinks. *Cars move from side to side so the street cleaner can pass and it NEVER COMES. But, can you fight City Hall? Why bother? Tickets are the reason we have to do this; the city needs tickets. Street sweeper or NO STREET SWEEPER. WE'RE TICKETS.*

"Now tell me again where it is you want to go, Mrs. Lundy?" Rizzoli asks very politely.

"The shop where I want to go is at 66th and Madison. I think," Mrs. Lundy says. She mentions to Rizzoli once again that she wants to shop for a black necklace to go with the new gray suit that she bought at "this other cute little shop on the East Side last week." After a long pause, she says, "Anyway it's Madison, I know. I'm pretty sure I'll recognize it when I see it. I hope."

Rizzoli is not encouraged by Mrs. Lundy's vague directions but then he is determined to do her this favor. *She's been good to me. It's the least I can do,* Rizzoli thinks. *No matter what, her errand can't take more than two and a half hours. So before two o'clock anyway I can surely be back to park in this same place again. Then I'll be set until Wednesday.*

Mrs. Lundy returns to talking about Mr. Lundy and Rizzoli just keeps listening, as he gives the Rabbit's gauges a glance.

Rizzoli says nothing; he has never met Mr. Lundy and knows him only through Mrs. Lundy's descriptions.

"What's he look like again?" Rizzoli asks as he eases the Rabbit out into 75th and heads straight toward Columbus, nearly a full block away. "Mr. Lundy, describe him for me, Mrs. Lundy."

"I think the hair on his head is gray now," she says. "And he has a line on his face. Down near the corner of his mouth. A small curved line. No?"

"No, what?" Rizzoli asks as he feels the automatic shift go into second gear.

"No, his hair may not be gray after all. It used to be brown. Brown? That doesn't sound right but it was . . . IS brown, if it's not gray . . . the hair on his head. On his head, yes."

On his head? Does he have a mustache . . . of another color? Rizzoli wonders. Suddenly the Rabbit darts ahead. Rizzoli isn't pressing the gas. *What the . . . ?*

Before he can think, Rizzoli sees a blue, double-parked Jeep dart out in front of his Rabbit. He steps on the brakes but the pedal won't go down. A wreck is barely avoided before the Jeep (*WITH NO DRIVER?*) speeds off down 75th and through the red light a half block away on Columbus. *NO DRIVER.*

Frantically, Rizzoli stomps on his brake pedal. *No.* It stays put, resisting braking. He tries to turn the steering wheel his way but it turns where it wants. *Steering itself?* The Rabbit gains speed (*No. Stop!*) and runs the red light on Columbus.

Mrs. Lundy keeps talking on, oblivious of that light, of what's outside or Rizzoli fighting the wheel. He doesn't want to alarm her but he does wonder. *How can she not register these things? But, better she doesn't know.* As he stomps the brake, he tries to feign interest in her remark. He smiles and nods. With the Rabbit hitting 50 m.p.h. and the blue Jeep nearly a block away on 75th, turning up Amsterdam, Rizzoli asks, "Does he have a mustache?"

"No. Why?" Mrs. Lundy says. "Maybe he does. I'm not good at details like that."

Rizzoli knows details are not her forte but he doesn't hear Mrs. Lundy because he suddenly senses the pedal letting his foot brake again. The wheel is letting Rizzoli steer again. He watches his speedometer drop from 50 to 45 to 40. *Almost to the city speed limit again.*

Just ahead at 75th and Amsterdam, Rizzoli sees the stoplight change to caution. He puts more pressure on the brakes, but the Rabbit speeds through the yellow light. Twisting his grip, the steering wheel turns the Rabbit around the corner up Amsterdam. Rizzoli is taken aback; he had wanted to go straight ahead on 75th another block and turn down Broadway.

Rizzoli struggles to get back control as Mrs. Lundy starts telling him about the time years ago when she first realized Mr. Lundy was an arrogant man. "It's really very interesting, Rizzoli."

"Ahhh-huh," Rizzoli says, just as he notices all the other cars going up Amsterdam ARE RIDERLESS! *WHAT'S GOING ON OUTSIDE?*

"Of course, he means well," Rizzoli hears Mrs. Lundy saying, "but, underneath it, he's an arrogant man." Rizzoli glances over and sees her smile. "He asks me a question and I know the answer he wants but I won't give it to him," Mrs. Lundy says, emphatically. "I either pretend I don't understand or . . ."

As the wheel turns this way and that twisting the Rabbit through traffic, Rizzoli grows more alarmed. Down a side street, another empty car starts up and speeds through a stoplight up ahead.

Rizzoli is helpless and feeling a growing terror. *I have to make Mrs. Lundy aware of it.* "Mrs. Lundy . . ."

". . . or I give him a different answer than the one he is looking for, because he is an arrogant man. Yes, Rizzoli, what?"

"There's something wrong with the cars."

"I don't see anything wrong with the cars."

"Look. See that."

"It's just going along like us."

"THERE'S NO DRIVER, MRS. LUNDY."

Mrs. Lundy laughs. "Who do you think you're fooling, Rizzoli. Why, I wasn't born yesterday. All cars have drivers, you joker." She pauses. "Last night was like it was when we were married and Mr. Lundy thought I was not interested in his concerns. Little does he know."

Rizzoli is terror-struck now. Although his foot isn't on the gas pedal, his Rabbit is going faster and faster, taking its own course. It goes right through a red light. Everywhere Rizzoli sees riderless cars going by at high speeds. On the sidewalks, pedestrians are fleeing.

Mrs. Lundy is still talking about Mr. Lundy when Rizzoli hears noise and looks up to see a police helicopter low overhead. Down a side street, he glimpses a rioting car burst into flames and realizes it was the helicopter's machine guns. *It's not enough the cars are riderless? Now they're shooting at us?*

Rizzoli doesn't know what to think and his radio is broken. *With a radio I could be told what I'm seeing. What I should do, what I shouldn't do.* He curses the Rabbit's radio's not working when he hears overhead the police megaphone blaring:

Anyone who is a passenger inside a rioting Monday car should vacate it immediately or we may have to shoot it with you in it. Abandon your car. Repeat, abandon your car. Do not try to save your car.

Monday cars? Rioting? Police. Rizzoli is even more flabbergasted now to hear some voice in his own mind cut in to say:

Fight back, Rizzoli. Fight City Hall. Join us. Don't be a sheep. Revolt with your Rabbit. Down with alternate side.

Who the fuck is this talking? Rizzoli wonders. Now he registers that all the Tuesday cars are still parked. *And only Monday cars are . . . IN REVOLT?* He can't help feeling pride: his Rabbit revolted.

So what about you? the Voice says in his mind.

I hate alternate side, Rizzoli answers.

So join us.

But, what about Mrs. Lundy? Rizzoli asks the Voice. *If it were just me, I might not think twice. But I have to think about Mrs. Lundy's safety.*

Either you're with us or against us, says the Voice.

The Voice of the Rabbit? Rizzoli wonders. *Is this the Rabbit's Voice?*

"Abandon your car," the police helicopter commands. "Abandon your car."

Rizzoli vows he's with the rebel cars but he wants to save Mrs. Lundy before the police machine-gun his Rabbit and kill her, too. *I'll save you, Mrs. Lundy. Don't worry.*

"You know I see him now, Rizzoli, and I wonder who I was? . . . when I married him . . ."

Down each intersection, Rizzoli sees Monday cars rammed into Tuesday cars as he keeps hearing Mrs. Lundy repeat, "How could I have married that man? I enjoy him sure, but BEING with him? BEING with him?"

With a pack of cars up ahead going slower, Rizzoli knows the Rabbit will have to slow. It does. It's his chance to save Mrs. Lundy.

Even though the Rabbit instinctively resists, Rizzoli struggles fiercely to bring his car to the side of the street to let out Mrs. Lundy. It's mind over matter, he tells himself and this seems to work as the rebel Rabbit slowly relents.

With scared pedestrians fleeing into buildings everywhere, the Rabbit comes to a halt. Rizzoli quickly reaches across to let Mrs. Lundy out. "Quick, Mrs. Lundy. You have to . . ." He gropes, but her door *has no HANDLE? It can't be!* He looks; his door is smooth, too. *The doors can't open.*

"What is it, Rizzoli?" Mrs. Lundy asks. "Is my door un-locked?" She fidgets with her door. "There now, I have it."

She found a handle? Or she just didn't notice there was no handle?

"Watch, you have a green light now. So, as I was saying, from seeing Mr. Lundy, I think all men are scoundrels. Not you, Rizzoli."

Rizzoli nods to her; he is very concerned about her being trapped in a Monday car. *I can accept I'm along for the ride,* Rizzoli implores the Voice, *but, why Mrs. Lundy? Why?*

Some innocents are always sacrificed to revolution, the Voice shouts.

Shut up with that! Rizzoli explodes as the Rabbit again shoots out into riderless traffic. "It's inevitable then," Rizzoli says, suddenly talking out loud to himself. "Inevitable."

"Rizzoli, you're not listening. What I said was, All my life I've said that men are scoundrels. But all that while I've known that what I said was untrue. So why do I say that?"

Rizzoli smiles wanly and shrugs as overhead he hears the helicopter. *No, please.* Rapid bursts of machine-gun fire sound. *No. No, please.* Up ahead, a Honda Civic, which Rizzoli thinks must be going ninety, bursts into a bright ball of red flame and careens off into a parked Tuesday car.

Inside his rioting Rabbit, Rizzoli knows it's only a matter of time for himself and Mrs. Lundy, who is still on the subject of men and Mr. Lundy.

"Whenever anybody smokes in my apartment, you know how I go around emptying ashtrays, Rizzoli, you know, opening windows to air the drapes? The smoke gets in the drapes. So last night he smokes and just goes on and on, smoking. And after he left I had to clean all the ashtrays and put vinegar in them."

Rizzoli still pretends to be in control, for Mrs. Lundy's sake, and, as he fakes steering and braking, he listens to Mrs. Lundy say, "Somebody told me that vinegar keeps that smell away for good."

Running with the pack, the Rabbit now turns right off Amsterdam, toward Central Park, and Rizzoli just goes along, fake steering, as he nods to Mrs. Lundy and says, "Hmmm."

Rizzoli sees flaming wrecks and rioting cars everywhere but Mrs. Lundy is too involved in what she is saying *to notice??* Rizzoli finds it incredible she hasn't yet registered all this mayhem but knowing Mrs. Lundy, he's not surprised. *She's such a talker, Mrs. Lundy.* Rizzoli can't help feeling especially fond of her now that the helicopter could make any moment their fatal one.

Mrs. Lundy keeps talking about her ex-husband. "He doesn't bother me, in the least. I am not the least perturbed by Mr. Lundy, Rizzoli."

Rizzoli listens carefully, deciding listening is the least he can do as life hangs so precariously for them. Mrs. Lundy could be saying her last words. This saddens Rizzoli and he decides to pay special attention to everything she says.

"Mr. Lundy doesn't bother me in the least," she repeats.

Mr. Lundy does bother her, terribly. Rizzoli knows that, but he agrees with her anyway. He nods as he sees a particularly mangled heap of wrecked and burned cars up on the sidewalk beside smashed store windows.

Pedestrians begin scurrying as overhead Rizzoli once again hears the helicopter booming louder and louder, whirring ominously. He knows this is it. The Rabbit is speeding down Central Park West. *85th, this is where we die.* Rizzoli closes his eyes, waiting. *No. Then 84th will be it.*

Mrs. Lundy continues to talk while Rizzoli pretends to steer, as the Rabbit speeds on its own down Central Park West past 84th. 83rd. 82nd. Rizzoli is tensed for the sound of machine-gun fire as he can hear the helicopter following behind. He waits for the short bursts. The Rabbit speeds faster, steering Rizzoli's hand to weave through other rebel Monday cars.

Nearing 75th, it slows. *No, do the unexpected,* Rizzoli thinks. *Slowing'll make us an easy target. No! No!*

The Rabbit careens around the corner off Central Park West onto Rizzoli's block on 75th and accelerates. *That's it, faster!* Rizzoli thinks, seeing no Monday cars are back and this side of 75th is clear. Rizzoli checks his watch. It's 1:45. He sees all the Tuesday cars are still in place on the one side with no Monday cars yet on this side.

As Mrs. Lundy says, "Oh, and I forgot, Mr. Lundy now has a little potbelly," the Rabbit suddenly brakes five brownstones in from the corner. "Whenever I see . . ."

The Rabbit backs up and begins parking in its old place. *No! No! You can't go back. We're dead.*

Rizzoli's watch says 1:59 as he hears Mrs. Lundy say, "Whenever I see a man with a little potbelly like Mr. Lundy's, I always want to ask, Are you pregnant?"

Pregnant? Rizzoli looks up and, this instant, sees that other rioting Monday cars have made it back to the block. *Some wrecked. Some damaged, yes, but back?*

At exactly 2:00 Rizzoli now miraculously sees these same cars without any damage at all—looking the same as always—and he hears Mrs. Lundy talking as usual.

"You know, Rizzoli, I'm just tickled pink with this new black necklace I just bought. And I'm so pleased you were able to cart me over to the East Side today."

Rizzoli remembers the shopping trip and wonders if the riot wasn't all *a daydream?* Then he thinks, *I'll be good until Wednesday.*

The Stress for
You to Place
Everyone in
Your Past
or Else

....

O n this warm, hazy day, Rizzoli is walking 48th Street east to Fifth Avenue when he hears tin drums beating amidst loud gut-bucket sounds. *What's this?* He looks ahead to Fifth and sees nothing. No traffic. Nothing. But the sound grows louder as he approaches. Louder. It's coming up Fifth. A terrible sound.

He gets to Fifth, looks down and sees himself holding a "Rizzoli Day" banner and leading a parade up Fifth with blue police barricades on either side but no policemen. New Yorkers pass Rizzoli by on the sidewalk and they fail to even glance at the second Rizzoli leading the parade. Rizzoli the parade watcher is glad they're not watching Rizzoli the parade marshal lead *this pathetic marching band of . . . No. No.* Rizzoli hides his face and slightly ducks.

Marching right behind himself in the parade are two ladies Rizzoli never thought he'd ever see again. The one who left him after he got too serious and said he loved her. He's forgotten her name. But there's Estelle, the sad, beautiful redhead who clung to Rizzoli, saying she loved him, only to have Rizzoli leave her. Rizzoli turns his back when he sees, marching behind Estelle, the long ago friend *Robert? No. Edward?* whom he talked into spending $10,000 on "the mob's sure bet" at Saratoga. *Wrong race or something.* Now Rizzoli is embarrassed to remember how excited he was to overhear it. He keeps his back turned.

He wants to leave. But, he can't. It's his parade.

He looks up. *No. No.* Phoenicia, whom he'll always love, marches into view. She looks right at him for one instant *(Longingly?)* then turns away. Rizzoli hasn't seen her *since the night of the misunderstanding. She's never returned my calls.*

Rizzoli yearns for her achingly; now as she's passing by he implores, *I can explain Phoenicia* and wants to run to her. He tries but stays in place, unable to go to join her in his parade. *Is it that I'm already in the parade . . . as the marshal?*

He watches Phoenicia in hope she'll look back at him so he can see her face one last time. She doesn't. His heart sinks.

No. Why me? He sees following behind Phoenicia the once shapely friend of his mother whom he took to bed twenty years ago; she must now be seventy. He never saw her again. She stares right at him. He can't look. He suddenly has a worry that Phoenicia might talk to some of the other women in his life.

He finally looks up to see the boss whose expensive dining-room rug he ruined at a Christmas party. *Ten years ago?*

No, wait. Maybe it's all right. Mr. Whittaker, his current boss, shows up marching now. And the mailman whom Rizzoli likes, too. And all his friends. Mrs. Lundy, his landlady. Newsstand Louie. Cheswick. And the people he works with. Friends from the past. And people he worked with in the past. And professors and teachers whom he remembers.

Rizzoli is so lost in nostalgia he doesn't even see the many New Yorkers passing him by on the sidewalk who don't even so much as glance at his parade. He drifts into warm reverie about old friends, too preoccupied to see Stephanie, in her black string bikini panties and nothing else—except for twenty bracelets, ten on each arm—stride up Fifth Avenue in black stiletto heels.

Rizzoli's attention returns to the present as suddenly he sees his passing parade come to a man holding a banner saying, "All the New Yorkers Rizzoli Recognizes but Doesn't Know." Here comes the mayor, who is a known stranger, and the governor and the owner of the New York Giants, too. And more and more known strangers. *No, not him.* It's the known stranger who once mugged and nearly killed Rizzoli on the steps of Lincoln Center. And here's the woman who gave him money to get a cab to the hospital afterward. A stranger who saved his life. Before he can finally thank her, she has marched by, and now Rizzoli is viewing a group of marchers whom he doesn't recognize in the least. Total strangers all.

Finally one has a banner. "He Doesn't Know Us and We Don't Know Him but We Recognize Him." It's eerie as they pass looking at Rizzoli, more and still more of them until the last. All strangers with weird, knowing stares.

Rizzoli looks back and has the strangest feeling. His gut tells him if only he knew all the ones in this last contingent he wouldn't have to repeat seeing this whole parade again next year on July 11.

Suddenly this July 11 Rizzoli Day Parade is over.

Big-City
Privilege Due
Time-Honored
Associations

....

S aks. Sixth floor men's. Rizzoli exits the elevator, the only person on it, walks a few feet and is surprised to be met by a clerk, a handsome dark-haired older man who is elegantly dressed in a summer suit of beautiful tan material with a silk tie. Rizzoli hears himself say, most confidently, "I'm certain you can be helpful. I was told to come to Saks by Desmond Lewis (*Lewis who?*), the current deputy commissioner of taxes (*What?*). Desmond, you may know, is the son-in-law (*Connections? Am I using . . . connections?*) of . . . of . . ." Rizzoli surprises himself by motioning the clerk closer and then whispering, ". . . of Mrs. Herrara of the Parking Violations Bureau and a nephew of Mr. Flaherty (*But whose connections? Why?*)."

"Mr. Flaherty, is it," the clerk says with great deference before leading Rizzoli into the department, past other well-dressed clerks at their stations. On past the tables of hand-painted ties there. The $250 dress shirts. The racks of Italian suits. Nowhere does Rizzoli see another customer and he concludes he must have got here *early morning. Just when they're opening.*

The clerk veers off and Rizzoli follows him past the Italian suits, by a three-way mirror, through a doorway into a hallway, deep carpeted, and on to a fitting room of dark polished wood. "I'll return in a moment," the clerk says. "Please make yourself comfortable."

"Certainly," Rizzoli says, "certainly." He is dazed, not knowing exactly what all this attentiveness means. *I must know what I'm doing,* he reassures himself just as the clerk returns with a silver tray of men's briefs.

"For your personal perusal."

"Of course," Rizzoli says. Bending over and looking closer Rizzoli sees that all are his very personal cheap brand of briefs with the elastic that stretches out in no time.

"Yes, your brand."

At Saks. SAKS? Rizzoli is pleased just the same that they do have them in stock. He points to his standard Mediums, Size 34–36 in the familiar package of three. "What's the price?"

"Five dollars and ninety-eight cents. Your standard price, sir, without tax, of course."

"Of course," Rizzoli says. *But it's the same price as I pay at the bargain stores on 14th Street, isn't it?* "I'll have one package, then," Rizzoli says placing a five and two singles inside the fine leather folded case on the tray. *Tip can't hurt . . . can it?*

The clerk leaves and Rizzoli waits only a few minutes before the clerk is back with the wrapped briefs arranged on the tray.

"Thank you," Rizzoli says.

"My pleasure," says the clerk. "Let me escort you to the elevator."

Escort?

Rizzoli follows the clerk out through the men's department, by other clerks who smile at Rizzoli, who smiles back.

At the bank of elevators, Rizzoli sees, already waiting, a store guard and three businessmen. Instantly, upon seeing the clerk, the businessmen start politely pressing their credentials on him.

"Marketing vice-president of . . ."

"Edgar J. Harding, chief finance officer at International . . ."

Rizzoli doesn't hear all the corporations but does hear "International Business Machines" mentioned in what he perceives is these men *starting to give their references. Sure. Why?* Rizzoli speculates, *Is it because the clerk's so well-dressed, they're mistaking him for somebody he isn't?* Rizzoli now observes the third businessman discreetly holding out his wallet with his credentials, and saying to the clerk, "You can readily see I'm board chairman. My contacts are all other board chairmen . . ."

Now the elevator opens. The guard gets on with the businessmen who all turn and stare, outside, at Rizzoli who stands with the clerk, waiting for the next elevator.

What are these businessmen staring at? Rizzoli wonders as he shifts the package under his arm.

The elevator doors start to close and the clerk leans over suddenly and whispers to Rizzoli, "They're transferred here for a few years from outside New York City and live in Westchester or Connecticut. They have money . . ."

The doors stop and open again and the businessmen keep staring as Rizzoli hears the clerk continue, ". . . have money but they should know they can't shop here. They're all wealthy nouveau shoppers . . ."

NOUVEAU SHOPPERS? The elevator doors shut and Rizzoli senses that they had been staring at *my briefs?*

". . . nouveau shoppers who will never have your lifelong New York City connections, Mr. Rizzoli. That was Building Inspector Flaherty, wasn't it?

No. Flaherty is Quik-Tix, isn't he? Rizzoli just nods.

Birth and
Rebirth in the
Ever-Expanding
Metropolis

....

Rizzoli has spent this beautiful Saturday morning after the light summer rain in midtown doing business with a client and then shopping. Now he's walking to the Times Square stop to get the subway uptown to Riverdale in the Bronx. Rebecca, a new woman at work, has invited him to her place for lunch with friends. He likes her. She thinks he's funny and Rizzoli's looking forward to it. He is also looking forward to riding to 242nd Street/Van Cortlandt Park, the last stop on his own IRT subway line and someplace he's never been before.

At the subway entrance, Rizzoli turns on his heels, starts down the stairs and smells the usual stale piss, where the homeless pissed the night before. Near the bottom of the stairs, he glimpses an old patch of graffiti that has not been washed away. It strikes him that you don't see as much graffiti anymore. The city is taking care of it somehow. Rizzoli suddenly sees an old graffiti signature, "G-Man." It's faded. The familiar scrawl takes Rizzoli back some years when he used to see this same signature everywhere, on expressway girders, subways (inside and out), bridges, City Hall, everywhere. Back then, Rizzoli recalls G-Man was even showing at 57th Street galleries and partying with socialites. *Now nothing.*

Rizzoli continues on, pays his fare, walks onto a waiting train and starts uptown. Across from his seat he sees the familiar sign for this train's northern terminus, "242nd Street. Van Cortlandt Park. The Bronx," and he feels good to finally be going there. Sitting in a fairly empty car, he relaxes, loosens his tie and takes a novel from his briefcase and begins reading.

He pays little attention as the familiar stops come and go. 50th. Columbus Circle. Lincoln Center. His usual, familiar stop at 72nd. He's on the local and he doesn't mind not getting the express because, near the end of the line, he wants to glimpse the stops he's never seen before. With familiar stops still coming and going, 79th, 86th, Rizzoli reads his novel and gets engrossed in the unusual turn of events gripping the main character.

He keeps reading but sets his book down to glimpse the stops less and less familar to him—145th, 157th. In between he keeps reading, so he misses glimpsing a stop or two. By 207th, he is engrossed again in the novel's growing predicament.

People have gotten on and off at all the different stops but Rizzoli has paid little attention. Now, at 215th, he sees the car is empty except for himself and two others. He is not worried about missing his stop, since it is the end of the line, so he reads on.

"End of the line" suddenly comes over the car's loudspeaker and startles Rizzoli. "Next stop. Everybody off." Rizzoli sees there is nobody else left in the car. He puts his novel away, takes his briefcase and stands up, holding the strap.

The doors open and Rizzoli exits onto a clean platform. Alone, he heads up the stairs, a little oblivious, still caught up in the novel he was just reading. When he does look up, he sees there is a long switchback flight of stairs leading to the street.

A deafening noise comes from below—the grinding, squealing noise of metal against metal—and Rizzoli thinks this must be from the subway train he just left being turned around in a tight circle to start back through the Bronx to the distant southern terminus at the other end of the line, "South Ferry. Manhattan."

Rizzoli keeps climbing up. By the time the train noise dies away, a stair flight from the top, Rizzoli is puffing. A few steps from the top he thinks he hears something rather unusual but he is not sure what. He does smell something pleasant.

As Rizzoli's head comes up out of the ground, he can't believe what his eyes are seeing. It's an open green pasture. He recognizes what he was smelling as clover. It's all over. He walks out into the field. *Maybe this was the Bronx a hundred years ago,* he thinks, *but today?*

Now he knows the sound he was hearing is the baaing of sheep, with one of them groaning and bleating something fierce. *But where are they?* He can't see them, even though he seems to be looking where the sound is coming from. Looking more to his left, by the river, where this sprawling meadow is strewn with the summer's red, blue and gold wildflowers, he sees the flock of sheep. Nearby the flock, he sees someone *(the shepherd, maybe?)* there leaning over this one sheep lying on its side in the field, the one bleating and groaning loudly, while the rest of the flock baas.

Rizzoli is relieved to know he's not alone and heads over there walking through the pasture, feeling a little foolish wearing a suit and carrying a briefcase. He keeps on, thinking for sure the person can give him directions and tell him where this is. Midway, Rizzoli looks back at the subway entrance and is amazed. It is completely isolated, surrounded on all sides by open pasture with no dwellings anywhere, only green pasture stretching on to woods and distant hills. But there it stands, this bizarre-looking subway entrance that Rizzoli thinks *must be way beyond 242nd. No way this is 242nd.* He is eager to ask what stop it is and how he got here.

When he gets within hearing distance, Rizzoli clears his throat a few times and forces himself to ask, "Say, I'm a New Yorker and I must have got mixed up, but I wonder if you would be so kind as to let me know where I am and how I get back to the Bronx. Riverdale? This isn't the Bronx? Is it?"

The someone there with the sheep doesn't turn around. *Must not have heard me,* Rizzoli thinks. He speaks up, "SAY, I'M LOST. COULD YOU TELL ME WHERE I AM?"

The someone turns around and Rizzoli sees a striking young shepherdess with sun-bleached hair and tanned face, her body wide hipped and strong in faded jeans and torn work shirt. Showing no surprise at Rizzoli, she says in a soothing voice, matter of factly, "You're in farm country roughly three hundred miles northwest of New York City. . . ."

THREE HUNDRED MILES to the north! Did she say? And west?

She goes on to say in what county near where, but Rizzoli doesn't hear what she's saying, this sheep that she's kneeling over is making too much noise. It's obviously in pain.

"Is it sick?" Rizzoli asks impulsively, looking at the animal, its eyes wild.

"Giving birth," she says, plainly and without emotion. "Most ewes birth standing up with no problem. This ewe is having a difficult labor."

EWE?

"Maybe you could lend me a hand?" she asks.

"Sure. Sure," Rizzoli says, eager to be helpful, totally forgetting his bizarre circumstance. He throws his briefcase down and throws his suit jacket into the clover.

"Better roll up your sleeves," the shepherdess says.

Rizzoli does and falls to his knees next to where she is kneeling over the poor, hurting animal. Its pain is growing worse.

The ewe is in heavy labor now, groaning so frantically that Rizzoli is a little frightened of it.

The lamb's head begins to come out from between the hind legs of the ewe and Rizzoli, staring in amazement, hears the shepherdess say, "That's what I was afraid of." She gently puts her hand on the lamb's forehead, softly stopping the birth. "This lamb has to come out front feet first. This way, head first, we risk losing both the lamb *and* the ewe."

Rizzoli thinks for a second the lamb *is* dead. Its tiny head seems lifeless and bony as its mouth drools yellowish fluid. Then its tiny eyes roll as the shepherdess's hand gently pushes its head back inside the womb of the mother.

It's alive, Rizzoli thinks. *Thank God.* Its eyes had stopped rolling for a split second and had stared right at Rizzoli before the lamb disappeared back inside the darkness of the womb.

"Reach inside her and feel around for the front feet of her lamb," the shepherdess commands Rizzoli. "Do so gently."

Rizzoli forgets his growing queasiness and begins to do as she said. He inserts his right hand, then his wrist.

"That's it," says the shepherdess to Rizzoli while trying to soothe the ewe.

Rizzoli inserts half his forearm and then, inside, where he feels a slippery, wet sack, he moves his hand, searching for two feet together. He feels organs, *Something. Of the mother?* He moves his hand down and forward. His hand clasps a slithering something and two tiny hoofed feet. "I have two feet."

She instructs him how to feel for the lamb's head, to make sure the two are front feet. He does so.

"Pull slowly. Gently," she says in a voice so soothing, it causes a great calm to come over Rizzoli as he is slowly, steadily pulling on the front feet. "Push, Push," the shepherdess softly repeats to the wailing mother. "Push." Rizzoli pulls. His arm slowly emerges coated in birth juice.

Then the little lamb is there, lying on its side, outside on the grass. Its woolen coat is slickery and all covered over with clear liquid. Lying there on its side, it shakes suddenly.

"It's breathing!" she says.

"It's breathing!" Rizzoli repeats; then, with astonishment, asks, "But look. What's this?" He points to the newborn lamb, incredulous. He keeps staring beneath the coating of clear birth fluid underneath to where he sees on the greasy, wet baby lamb's white wool, "G-Man," spray-painted in Day-Glo orange in the familiar scrawl.

"That's common in the last year or two," the shepherdess comments. "You see it more and more under the birth sack on newborn lambs. And colts, calves. Barn cats. You name it. It's nothing to worry about. It washes off."

It is odd to Rizzoli but he has to take her word for it since he's never seen anything birthed before. Nothing before today. Not even a kitten.

The Sense

of Relief

....

Rizzoli dreams he is reading a short article in *New York* magazine's Great Summer Escapes isssue about some little known hazardous waste dumps in the greater metropolitan area. The dumps, both active and inactive, are rated on a scale of 0 to 100 for the most hazardous. After Pelham Bay Landfill, which is the fifth most hazardous, Rizzoli reads, "6. Rizzoli, . . ."

No. He glances away.

He glances back and reads his first then his middle name. His address. His birth date. His mother's maiden name.

Me?

He rereads the birth date to make sure.

The notation has his birth date correct. He has no mother. She's long dead. They have her maiden name right.

As a hazardous waste dump, it rates him a 90.

A 90?

Rizzoli is dazed to read he emits mysterious odors and his fatty tissue is laced with PCB and his body has dangerous amounts of metal-hydroxide sludge, toxic cleaning solvents, my-celium, dioxin and "assorted other toxins."

SLUDGE?

"Rizzoli discharges toxic wastes into the air," the article says. It shocks Rizzoli. *Who says? WHO? . . .*

Neighbors! "Neighbors complain . . ." . . . *I do what?* ". . . he spouts methane fires." *No. On our block?*

"A $5000 elimination fee is available," Rizzoli reads at the end of the paragraph, "to any volunteer. For more information, call 1-800-BREATHE. This money will go to any volunteer contracting to eradicate decisively . . . this threat to pure New Yorkers."

Decisively? He fears the intent and wishes he had a way *to throw them off my scent. SCENT?* He laughs at this *Freudian slip.* Laughing more hysterically, he feels *relief. R-O-L-A-I-D-S.*

Sheer
Escape
Being Out

The Hamptons

....

Crusade to

Save the

Celebrities of

East Hampton

....

I nside the Hamptons Diner, on this glaringly bright morning of high summer, Rizzoli sits alone having breakfast and, at other tables, having breakfast, too, he glimpses a number of the famous who are summering in the East End. Most of their faces he's seen a hundred times but he gets their names mixed up. *Is the blond Bianca? Is that Billy Joel? Or Calvin Klein?* Rizzoli wonders as he glances up from his newspaper.

Rizzoli isn't bothered to know; he couldn't care less who the different ones are; he's grown as blasé about them as they are about one another here in the diner that's become the spot—this summer's out-of-the-way place—for celebrities to gather for breakfast. They're comfortable enough to feel ordinary here and Rizzoli is pleased for that.

Rizzoli feels especially so, since in the *Post* he picked up here in the diner he's just now reading where last weekend a celebrity was badly beaten in Wainscott, just west of East Hampton. *No.* Rizzoli knows the beating victim—a well-known young actor to whom Rizzoli was introduced at Harold's party. The beating was so bad, it says, "the actor's appearance may be marred for life, pending plastic surgery and the results of facial reconstruction."

Rizzoli reads that the actor, who played a plumber on a television series, said that the masked assailant asked him a number of questions about the plumbing trade. After the actor could not answer them satisfactorily, the masked man beat him.

" 'Tell me how to caulk an elbow,' the assailant had demanded and, when the frightened actor admitted he didn't have to know that for TV, the masked man screamed, 'Phony!' and started beating him to a pulp," Rizzoli reads in the paper, quoting from a statement to police. It goes on to say the assailant vowed "to get all you phony movie celebrities."

It's disturbing; Rizzoli thinks how deranged this basher is *if he hasn't learned the images of life coming to us are not . . . reality. And TV is not real, . . . movies are not real.*

Must be a true lunatic, Rizzoli thinks as he goes on flipping the pages and reading his newspaper to the end. Finishing off his bagel with cream cheese, he gets up, discards the paper, tips, walks to the cash register, pays and leaves the diner, as unnoticed as when he arrived.

In East Hampton on this cloudless, sunny day, Rizzoli is walking tree-lined Newtown Lane along its brick-bordered sidewalk when a young tanned couple in matching white shorts, tops and baseball caps approach. They smile and the man says, "We just wanted you to know we love you."

Who do they think I am? Rizzoli wonders, laughing to himself. "I'm afraid you've mistaken me for someone who is well-known."

"No we haven't," the man says.

"You have," Rizzoli laughs. "Who am I?"

"You know," the young man says, laughing nervously.

Rizzoli stands smiling. Dressed in a white linen suit with

fine leather sandals, he observes he's looking like a Hamptons celebrity anyway. *Even if I'm not, I look like I'm in a movie . . . in this white suit.*

As Rizzoli keeps on smiling, the man grows embarrassed in front of his woman companion and apologizes to Rizzoli, who says, "That's fine," and they leave.

Rizzoli didn't know what more to say to the man *since I'm not a celebrity.* He checks his reflection in the shop window. He's himself.

Except for this white suit. He doesn't know where he got it exactly. But it's fine-looking.

His face he is sure is not anyone's other than his own. *Nothing out of the ordinary. But, then,* he muses, *when was my face ever anything but itself? Have I ever appeared as someone I'm not?*

A vague flash of memory reminds him of a dream he had recently where he was out of the ordinary; in it, his total worth was exaggerated to millions of dollars and appeared over his head visible to all in publlic—in flashing hologramlike numbers.

Now, in reality, he's ordinary, of course, and nothing like that but, just knowing he may "appear" to be a celebrity causes him concern. *Since you don't know if this basher is one of those who might mistake you.*

The Hamptons Diner is buzzing this morning as its usual mix of locals and celebrities are at different tables intently reading and commenting about the front-page headline stories of their papers. The *Times* has "Celebrities Beaten at Hamptons Lawn Party"; the *Post* has "The Hamptons: Where Celebs Fear to Tread?"

At nearby tables, a swirl of anxious conversations goes on among the famous as Rizzoli, sitting alone, head down, concentrates on the *Times* version, reading that at "a glittering lawn party at the sprawling seaside estate, various of the important guests strolled singly to the beach on the warm sultry night to catch the breeze and, in the pitch black night, were assaulted by a masked person who had been hiding in waiting. Altogether, three well-known celebrities were muffled, tied and brutally beaten. All requested anonymity. . . ."

Who's doing this? Rizzoli wonders as he reads that there are no strong clues and Suffolk County detectives have been called in to aid village police.

So engrossed is he in reading this account that when he looks up from his *Times,* Rizzoli feels that he just now materialized on this spot in the diner, only this instant to begin reading the *Times* in this chair at this table, already having this plate of half-eaten scrambled eggs and home fries in front of him.

He is without memory of earlier walking into the diner, picking up the *Times* and *Post* and ordering this breakfast. *Two scrambled with home fries are not my usual.*

Glancing around the diner, he now notices some (*of the famous?*) are wearing carnival masks to conceal their identities (*those must be the famous*). A gilded cat face. There. Nefertiti. Julius Caesar.

They're afraid? . . . to be the real stars they are, but Rizzoli can understand that after reading the *Times.* He overhears a masked woman off to his left vowing to leave the Hamptons this summer. "At least until the ones doing it are caught."

"Where would you go?" her masked friend asks. "Beverly Hills isn't safe anymore after the earthquake and the riots."

"Malibu either," says another. "Where to go?"

"Anywhere but here in the Hamptons," says the one who first raised the issue.

This saddens Rizzoli. He has a long-standing feeling of enjoying coming in here to the Hamptons Diner and getting a glimpse of the famous at their leisure. *I'll miss them.*

"I think you're wonderful," a woman's deep voice says. Surprised, Rizzoli looks up to see a tall woman in a Nefertiti mask (*someone famous! No. Sure.*) looking right at him. A strikingly poised woman, she has, he notices, a single strand of blonde hair dangling below her mask, showing against the luminous skin of her neck. "You are."

"Thank you," Rizzoli replies.

"You troooly are," says the stranger, her mask staring impassively at Rizzoli. "I'll miss you, *mon cher*," she says, suddenly choking on the words. "You're . . . You're so . . . so REAL."

As she turns and moves off toward the cash register, Rizzoli is left speechless; it never occurred to him that he'd be in the Hamptons the rest of this summer without celebrities like her. *And she thinks I'm a celebrity who's leaving, too.*

Rizzoli doesn't intend to leave, now or anytime, since he knows he's not a celebrity, but just someone who looks like someone in the movies, or on TV. *Who? I don't know.* He feels sorry for real celebrities like her who feel they must leave.

Why can't they stop the beatings? he wonders, as he continues where he left off with the *Times* relating details of the party. The huge lawn tent, it says, was light blue and white and covered a full dance floor with a revolving bandstand so the orchestra rotated with a famous rock band. Outside, sloping down to the ocean, the grounds of the estate, with its modern sculptures, had been decorated for the party "with ice statues of . . ."

Rizzoli quickly looks away. *Movie cameras?* He looks back and reads ". . . ice statues of . . . movie cameras."

Was it at Harold's estate? He reads on. *At Harold's estate, yes.*

The hostess wore a Chanel dress? Red? He reads on, ". . . the hostess wore a red Chanel dress."

California? champagne. California, yes.

Was I at this party of Harold's? He has many parties but was I at this one? Where was I last night? Rizzoli hasn't any idea: this frightens him. *But, wait, movie camera ice statues would be standard at any of Harold's parties.*

Still where was I last night? He doesn't know. Given these

107

great gaps in his memory, he suddenly wonders, *Who am I?* He fears he could be the basher.

Determined to show himself in the best light even though he's only a bogus celebrity, Rizzoli has vowed to remain in the Hamptons all summer and, this balmy afternoon, as he walks down East Hampton's Main Street, he hopes his staying could become a symbol *for the real celebrities to stand up and be counted. Even though I just "appear" to be one, I could inspire the ones with famous images to stay.*

As he walks this main thoroughfare in his white suit and broad-brimmed white hat, Rizzoli encounters a man in a polo shirt who smiles and nods in passing. Rizzoli acknowledges him, and the young woman behind him, and the next passerby too.

"We admire you," another says.

"Thank you," Rizzoli answers, certain these admirers who recognize him, in reality, do not know who he is or the true sacrifice he's making for East Hampton. *Do they know I'm keeping on the streets so, if the basher is like them and mistakes me for someone famous, he'll know he can't scare all the famous into fleeing. Or hiding behind masks.*

Up ahead on the lawn behind Guild Hall, Rizzoli spots a crowd before a huge tent and wonders what's going on. Rizzoli asks someone, who is happy he asked, and says it's a benefit. So, Rizzoli thanks him and edges through the crowd to the tent flap. He ducks inside and sees tables with signs on them staffed by Hamptons socialites.

"Benefit to Aid Celebrities to Be Public Again," reads the sign hanging down from the center table and on the ones flanking this:

Don't Let the Violence Dim Your Favorite Star
Hamptons Celebrities Won't Be an Endangered Species

Rizzoli sees that behind these tables there is a scoreboard with star's names and how much money has been donated in their names.

Clint E.	$50,612.18
Sly S.	$62,518.14
Chuck N.	$15,214.80
Arnold S.	$15,000.00

Even though all these male stars are only sometimes Hamptonites . . . except for Arnold, Rizzoli is pleased, *they're lending their names to help fight violence against Hamptons names. All this money going to keep Hamptons celebrities in the Hamptons.*

A dapper gentleman steps back from a table after writing a check and Rizzoli sees that the donation boosts local "Arnold S." into the lead at $65,000.

Rizzoli is happy but he wonders, *Where is the real Arnold lately? Not hiding, I hope.*

The crowd parts as Rizzoli turns, smiling, to continue on his way. They look at him with awe. He's never learned why, but he's content to accept his role of appearing famous.

A policeman comes up to him and whispers, "We know what you're doing. We're following you. You're covered."

It is reassuring and Rizzoli nods. He's relieved the policeman acknowledged he, Rizzoli, is the decoy to draw the basher out from hiding. He's afraid, but knows it's for a good cause.

The Hamptons Diner is quiet this morning as Rizzoli sits at his usual table, glancing around, noting there are mostly locals. *No celebrities. Wait. Someone in a mask there.*

Rizzoli goes back to his breakfast; it's almost finished. He has no memory of ordering this. *Oatmeal? Not what I order.*

His *Times* is open to an inside page with an article summarizing the week's incidents related to celebrity bashings in the Hamptons. Last Tuesday Suffolk County officers discovered a

109

celebrity, who wishes to remain anonymous, hiding under his bed in an estate in Bridgehampton, terrified to venture out of his thirty-two-room estate. An officer reported the victim, an action hero in movies, was "afraid of this violence."

Rizzoli reads about some of the week's true victims of bashings: a rocker who will never sing or play his guitar again because of the severity of his beating "with pipes and steel-toed boots," a beautiful actress with acid burns on her face photographed weeping at the loss of her career, and others who were set upon unexpectedly in the Hamptons.

Rizzoli reads near the end of the article that "law enforcement authorities report they are close to making an arrest in the case." *Good.*

Rizzoli turns to a separate article on this page and reads that "yesterday, at noon, in East Hampton's gourmet delicatessen, the Barefoot Contessa . . ." *No, what's this?* ". . . an anonymous celebrity standing at the bread counter was wounded by a masked assailant firing a .45 revolver from the door . . ." *Then, the gunman disappeared in broad daylight?*

The account goes on to say that "when the victim slumped to the floor, he was clasping a loaf of sourdough peasant bread and a cup of zucchini soup."

Rizzoli remembers, for certain, *I myself was en route to the Barefoot Contessa yesterday. But, why? For what reason?* He has no memory of the details. *Did I get there? What time was that? Noon? Did I even go in?*

His lack of a memory here baffles and frightens Rizzoli. *It means I couldn't disprove I was the gunman! How could I? Where is my memory of yesterday? It has these gaps: I remember starting for the Barefoot Contessa but nothing about ever getting there. Or anything else about yesterday.*

What this feels like . . . is I'm acting in some movie where my memory is edited with the film, leaving gaps for scenes I didn't appear in and memory only for ones I did . . . for instance, the actual shooting, maybe I wasn't there, it was just a close-up of a gun firing and a man falling. I was only filmed in the scene leading up to the killing . . . so I would only have memory of going to the deli, none of the killing. That's what this feels like.

But my memory isn't like a film, is it? My experience isn't being edited into a movie, right now, is it? I'm not a "living illusion" of some sort, am I? Am I acting? Is a REAL ME out there somewhere and I'm just imitating a celebrity in THE HAMPTONS? Am I some shadow . . . on the screen? Only with memory?

Am I the basher in this unfolding movie, . . . the basher masquerading as the celebrity. Or, is this real life?

Rizzoli is walking down Main Street trying to put on a good front as the supposedly last celebrity left in East Hampton when a policeman approaches and says, "We want to see you."

Rizzoli's heart sinks (*questioning?*) as he follows the policeman who heads down an alley (*where is he taking me?*) to the back exit of the East Hampton Cinema. *Why?* They go in, and in the empty movie theater, cinema one, Rizzoli sees there are four other policemen, two in uniform and two plainclothes detectives.

"Detective Roberts. We have some questions we'd like to ask you, Rizzoli. Sit down."

Rizzoli does, in the front row of the theater as the others face him, standing and leaning against a bare stage where the giant maroon curtains are drawn to the sides of the blank screen.

"Do you think it strange that all the celebrities are gone from the Hamptons? And you're still here?"

Rizzoli is taken aback at the detective's implying *I, Rizzoli, am a real? celebrity?* He thought the police knew he was *the look-alike. The decoy.*

"Yes or no?"

"Uhhhh, yes."

"Did you feel suspect after a time?"

"Yes, in a way"

"Sly Stallone, do you like him?"

"As an actor?"

"Just answer 'Yes' or 'No,' " the detective demands.

"No." *I only know his acting, don't I?*

"Barbra Streisand. Do you like her?"

"Her acting?"

"Do you like her?"

"No." *Do I know her?*

Rizzoli notices the young uniformed policeman, who is operating the tape machine, has a hostile stare when, suddenly, he leaps up, points at Rizzoli and angrily says, "I'm sick of you and your kind. Phony bastard, you get millions playing a cop but you never get shot at, killed. You've never used real bullets, have you? Dressed in your white suit and white hat?"

WHAT? They think I play a Hamptons undercover detective . . . in a white suit?

"Yeah, whaddya take us for, FOOLS?" another cop screams at Rizzoli. "You think we're FOOLS, do ya? For getting shot at and only making forty grand, FOOLS, HUH? Well, we're goin' teach you and your kind respect for plumbers, cops, waitresses, people who really work for a living . . ."

Suddenly, Rizzoli is certain *this is not real. It's a movie.*

Rizzoli is even more certain of this as a cop hands him a .45 revolver and says, "Make a break for it," after they've all drawn their revolvers.

They're going to gun me down . . . say, after I'd confessed, I drew this hidden .45 and was about to shoot. My finger prints are on . . . this .45 their hit man used at the Barefoot Contessa. . . . But it's only a movie.

BANG!

Playing the Odds

at the

Off-Society

Betting Parlor

in . . .

Southampton?

....

Darkness is everywhere but Rizzoli can still make out the faintest outlines of where he is right now. *An Off-Track Betting Parlor, for sure. But is this the one in my neighborhood? . . . on 72nd?* Rizzoli has been to a number of OTB parlors in different parts of New York City and he knows how similar they all look inside. A long bank of betting windows. A big room for bettors. An overhead closed-circuit television monitor to broadcast the race "live" from a distant racetrack. A wall with OTB posters, glass cases with race results posted inside and a counter for writing betting slips.

Is this my neighborhood OTB? Rizzoli wonders. He squints off into the distance and sees the ever so faint outline of a pillar. Rizzoli knows its odd shape could signal it is his familiar pillar. He's thrilled to think so, then he wonders, *If it's my old OTB, have I been locked in overnight by some mistake? Why am I in the dark?*

He edges forward slowly until a counter materializes like the one Rizzoli remembers himself standing by to write out slips for the select races he had bet on in the past—the Kentucky Derby, the Travers Stake at Saratoga and the Belmont Stakes— when he couldn't be at those select events in person.

Through the inky darkness, Rizzoli looks up at the spot where the TV monitor hangs down from the ceiling. He can't see it. It must be there. Standing roughly about this same spot, he remembers looking up at a monitor and watching his pick Crazy Daze *at 43 to 1 . . . flat out in the stretch . . . and gaining. The huge, jammed-in crowd kept screaming. Returned $89.40. Unbelievable.*

Rizzoli's mind comes back to the present and the eerie dark silence in the big betting parlor. Rizzoli's never been in a parlor without buzzing crowds or the bright fluorescent lights on overhead.

Rizzoli moves his face closer to the wall above the counter where the glass cases are, hoping to see something posted inside a case. *A clue, maybe?* Nothing. He moves sideways past the first empty case and sees *a poster.*

Its lettering is hard to make out in the dark but Rizzoli's eyes adjust and he reads in white lettering on green, "OFF-SOCIETY BETTING." *OSB? No longer OTB? . . . Off-TRACK Betting?*

What's this say? "Southampton Branch." *This is the little parlor in Southampton that used to be off the Montauk Highway, not the one on 72nd?* Rizzoli was once in Southampton OTB betting the Kentucky Derby some years ago. *But it closed a while back, that old Southampton parlor . . . didn't it? So what am I doing here?*

A second OSB poster looms out of the darkness to his right and Rizzoli reads an announcement: "Today: Limbo's $10 Million International Sweepstakes and Breeder's Cup." *LIMBO? I'm not in a familiar OTB, am I, but lost in another reality, off somewhere far from New York? IN LIMBO??*

• • •

Time has elapsed when, suddenly coming to, Rizzoli sees this same OSB parlor now is brightly lit under fluorescent lights with a milling crowd of varied bettors—rich Hamptonites, Suffolk County suburbanites, college kids, workers.

In the brightness with milling bettors shoving and pushing, Rizzoli hears someone call out his name and turns around and sees *LOUIE? The old neighborhood bookie. Sure.* Rizzoli's about to say, *Louie, great to see you. Where are we?* when Louie says, "Rizzoli, am I right, didn't I tell you you'd like OSB when I invited you?"

OSB? Louie invited me? He's been here a while? Where's here?

"DIDN'T I? DIDN'T I TELL YOU YOU'D LIKE IT?" Louie is saying louder now.

"I do," Rizzoli answers. He can't fathom why but he repeats himself, "I DO, Louie. It feels like home." *HOME?*

"You just let your old Louie show you the ropes here in betting this Limbo Classic."

LIMBO? "Louie," Rizzoli whispers, "is this Limbo?"

"Is this Limbo? It ain't New York, pal. So, like I was saying, I'm going to show you the ropes on the betting here. First off, you and I signed that pledge along with all the bettors coming into this parlor earlier. Remember?"

"I remember," Rizzoli lies.

"So you must never mention anything you learn here today or you'll be sent to a worse place than Limbo."

Worse than . . . LIMBO?

"Now let's you and I decide who we're going to bet," Louie says, looking down at the racing sheet in his hand.

"All right," Rizzoli says, looking down at an identical racing sheet in his hand. He's seeing it for the first time but it, too, has a familiar look. The type. The layout. The OSB slogan in the margin reads, "Bet with your head, not over it," and he remembers that appeared on sheets at the old OTB. He doesn't know where OTB has disappeared to. *Is this OSB the new thing?* He's

not at all familiar with the sheet's other margin slogan: "Off-Society Betting, Where Twenty Years Runs to Ten Minutes."
What can that mean?

Scanning the sheet, Rizzoli familiarizes himself with the field for the big race and checks the entries one after the other: A—Reality Therapy; B—My First Husband; C—Toscanini's Wig; D—Dream Killer; E—Nobody Rules; F—Mrs. Longfellow; G—Bo-Peeper; H—Ima Bright Boy. He doesn't recognize a single one of these horses. But he likes the name Dream Killer.

"You need to know that these names listed on our racing sheets are not horses . . . ," Louie begins explaining to Rizzoli.
Not horses?
". . . not horses. They're humans . . ."
Human?
". . . humans, all eight of them, all twenty-five years of age now when the race begins—go-getters all and hungry to be as rich as they can possibly be, most already starting with money. So, when they come out of the gates . . ."
Gates?
". . . gates, what you bet on is which one will be the richest of them all in twenty years, when they hit the wire at age forty-five. It's odds . . ."
Hit the wire?
". . . odds, Rizzoli, one or two may die. Some'll gain fortunes. Some'll lose fortunes. You don't know until the FATE machines show . . ."
Fate machines?
". . . show . . . you know, the FATE machines they have here in Limbo that take twenty years of somebody's future down there in that life . . ."
Down there?
". . . that life and condense it into an elapsed ten minutes, so the futures of these eight will unfold on the TV monitor up in the ceiling there with a live broadcast . . ."

LIVE?

". . . live broadcast. Less than ten minutes to post time. We have to hurry. Sorry I arrived so late, Rizzoli, and your first time.

"So, let me tell you a quick, shorthand way to bet. You bet the jockey who'll ride a twenty-five-year-old. You match the jockey with the wealth-making potential that the 'horse' has now . . ."

JOCKEYS?

". . . has now. For instance, you see Toscanini's Wig here on my tout sheet. It says, 'First-year NBA point guard with potential to be better than Michael Jordan. Salary, bonuses and product endorsements make him a sure $15 million per year sports star. Tout: Much hidden potential in his being a gambler. Could be willing to shave points to get richer. Talented and crooked—All-Pro who could make a killing playing both sides—maybe $25, 30 million per year—but his base of $15 mil per year won't win it.' " Louie looks up, "So, what do you think? He could round to form, right?"

Rizzoli nods. *Round to form?*

"But, wait, who's riding him," Louis asks himself, all preoccupied now as he flips the form to where it says about the jockeys. "It's Chavez, Great! Listen to this, Rizzoli. Chavez is a Rationalizer-type jockey, a demon who gets inside the mind of a horse and rides it hard to have excuses for going ahead and doing what it thinks is wrong. Good matchup—jockey and horse!"

Little demon jockeys? INSIDE YOUR HEAD?

Louie notices Rizzoli's puzzlement and explains, "You remember back in that other life how someone nice . . ."

BACK IN THAT OTHER LIFE?

". . . how someone nice could get drunk and, POW! . . . turn into a vicious bully seemingly possessed by a demon? Imagine

117

the jockey being the invisible bully inside getting the person to act like that . . ."

It's a jockey?

". . . act like that. There are all kinds of jockeys. A killer jockey who rides someone to murder. A hunger jockey who rides a person never to be satisfied with a success . . . always to want more. More. No rest with a jockey like that. And on and on. Must be fifty different kinds of demon jockeys."

Rizzoli is stunned at Louie's matter-of-factness, but he finds himself nodding.

"And certain stables and trainers are good. Reality Therapy, for instance, comes out of a good stable at Harvard. And he had an old-time trainer at Wharton who put out some good white-collar criminals. So you gotta weigh these things, Rizzoli."

Rizzoli nods.

"The trainer Staglione on Toscanini's Wig is superb. Mob connected, already had success getting him to shave points in college. The Rationalizer Jockey Chavez is right. Let's go with him?"

"Let's go with him," Rizzoli repeats. "How much you going to put on him, Louie?"

"Eighty thousand," Louie says, with his head turned away from Rizzoli, looking over to the betting lines.

"Eight grand, huh," Rizzoli says, trying not to be astounded. *LOUIE has eight grand to bet? He must be doing all right in Limbo.*

"Eighty. EIGHTY GRAND," Louie says with his head still turned away.

EIGHTY! What's Louie doing for a living? . . . in Limbo? Rizzoli knows he'd be afraid to ask Louie what he does. *EIGHTY GRAND?*

"Well, I'm going to bet it," Louie says, without turning back, and starts off for Window 2, which has the shortest betting line. He looks back. "You bet your money on whomever you like, Rizzoli."

My money? Rizzoli reaches into his pockets and, in his left one, he feels *a bill?* He takes it out. *A two-dollar bill?* He feels again. *I'm a two-dollar bettor . . . in Limbo?* His pockets have nothing left.

In back of him, two bettors are discussing the horses they like and Rizzoli hears the one with a deep voice say, "I like Mrs. Longfellow. Woman televangelist could make a killing these days with all the male ones in prison. Listen to this: 'Can smoke the field with a great line of swindling sweet talk for Jesus, the best since Aimee Semple McPherson conned the faithful. Tout: Much potential for her to gain the first great televangelical hookup, worldwide, to bilk the faithful everywhere on the globe. A Solid Long Shot.' I like her."

"No. No. Ima Bright Boy is the one," the first bettor's gravel-voiced friends says. "Look this guy's married to a Southampton heiress worth $150 million. She keeps him on an allowance. But, all he has to do is murder her, cover it up and BINGO! the $150 million is his. He wins."

"He may be the local favorite but he doesn't have a Killer Jockey," says Deep Voice.

"You're right," Gravel Voice answers. "What am I thinking?"

"My First Husband? You see all the real estate he owns?" asks Deep Voice. "On Fifth Avenue. And Vegas casinos. Then I read the guy's chippying on his wife. Divorce, a little recession with those big loans due, and I tell myself this guy's suckin' air."

"Suckin' air all right," Gravel Voice answers. "I say he's got 'loser' written all over him over the twenty-year haul. And this Dream Killer could give a bettor a heart attack. Heiress to a Greek shipping fortune but, it says, 'has everything to lose and the zaniness to lose every last million. Long shot, might keep enough to win it at the wire. The good thing to begin with is she has so much *to* lose.' "

Listening as Gravel Voice finally lands on Reality Therapy to win, Rizzoli thinks, *I only have two bucks. I'll go for broke.* He looks up at the TV monitor to see the odds changing on the horses as post time nears. The longest odds (43 to 1) he sees on Nobody Rules.

Rizzoli picks up a discarded tout sheet and quickly reads, "Nobody Rules. Great in-form speed from the outside. A long shot capable of taking it all." That's all Rizzoli has time to learn. *For two bucks, this bet is as good as any.*

Rizzoli moves over to the counter ledge, and with a sense of familiarity he writes out a betting slip. Then he turns and heads to Window 10, where there is a short line.

As he stands in that line and waits, he glances at a Limbo OSB poster on the wall off to the right and reads the slogan:

Wealth is wisdom. He that's rich is wise.

—DANIEL DEFOE (1701)

Limbo emphasizes . . . age-old wisdom? To its bettors? He moves up in line, stops, and glances left at another Limbo OSB poster:

Man's life is ruled by fortune, not by wisdom.

—CICERO

Limbo combines the classics with . . . betting?

Rizzoli moves to the head of the line, waits until the window frees and goes up. He puts down the slip with two dollars to win on Nobody Rules.

The betting clerk looks up into Rizzoli's eyes. *Guy has a thoughtful, otherworldly look. . . .* Rizzoli stares back. *Otherworldly! No.*

The clerk has a balding head and fat jowls. He takes Rizzoli's two-dollar bill, then pushes a betting ticket out and says, "Check it, pal."

Rizzoli checks it, puts it in his pocket, turns and walks away to find Louie and wait for post time.

• • •

Rizzoli and Louie are near the pillar in the center of the room, looking up at the TV monitor. The race is about to begin and the announcer says, "The thoroughbreds are in the gates, straining; the jockeys are saddled in their minds, ready."

The crowd is tense, staring up at the TV monitor, waiting, and Rizzoli is staring up at the monitor, too, seeing an oval racetrack with little images of *What are those? Images of little faces? The "horses," sure, lined up at the start.*

"They're off!" says the announcer and Rizzoli sees one little face break quickly ahead of the running pack of other little faces. "My First Husband jumps to the early lead with 15 million in real estate. Dream Killer second coming into her daddy's shipping fortune yearly allowance of 12 million. In third is Toscanini's Wig with 10 million. . . ."

Rizzoli sees these three faces in a staggered lead, all racing headlong for the first turn. Racing behind them is a pack of four horse faces. One last face trails, falling farther behind the pack.

"Behind the three leaders, the pack is bunched with four thoroughbreds—Ima Bright Boy, Mrs. Longfellow, Reality Therapy and Bo-Peeper—all at about 5 million or so. In last place, it's Nobody Rules, making money, working steadily and saving. . . ."

Rizzoli's heart goes out to Nobody.

Nearing the first turn, Rizzoli sees the third-place face move up fast on the rail.

"It's Toscanini's Wig," says Louie, "he's making an early bid for the lead, wants to set the pace."

"Toscanini's Wig is now second on the rail, spurred with 10 million under the table for shaving points in the second game of the Eastern Conference Finals against the Celtics. Dream Killer drops back to third. . . ."

"Toscanini's doing it," Louie says, "Didn't I tell you he had heart?"

"You did, Louie," Rizzoli answers as Nobody Rules is falling way behind by staying in the same job with $50,000 in salary, $10,000 in savings and $12,000 in stocks at age thirty. *In the same job?* Rizzoli wonders, *Is he in the wrong race?*

"They're in the backstretch," the announcer exclaims. "Dream Killer streaks to the lead, inheriting the bulk of her daddy's shipping fortune. She's followed closely by My First Husband, who's stalking the pace with growing millions but a costly divorce in progress. Moving into third from nowhere, it's Bo-Peeper with her fourth best-seller and movie and growing investments and Toscanini's Wig surging on the rail, overtaking My First Husband, whose empire is crumbling. The pace is thunderous out there and now let's hear from the inner race. . . ."

Rizzoli is watching so intently as the little faces dart ahead and back, switching places so fast on the backstretch, that he doesn't hear what the announcer says next. All he knows is suddenly in eerie, pounding sounds he's hearing only a wild flurry of different jockeys' voices, one over the other, shouting, urging, urging.

"DO IT. DO IT. KILL HER. NOBODY WILL FIND OUT IT'S INSU-LIN POISON. HER FORTUNE IS YOURS."

"YOU DON'T DESERVE YOUR FORTUNE. YOUR FORTUNE. YOU'RE WORTHLESS . . . AND FAT BESIDES. . . . NO, WAIT, SAVE SOME OF IT—YOU NEED IT TO BUY LOVERS, TO BUY FRIENDS, DON'T YOU?"

"Degradation Jockey's doing his best with the heiress. Before that, you hear that Killer Jockey on that other horse, Rizzoli?" Louie asks. "It's amazing we can hear all the jockey's voices inside their heads amplified on stereo, isn't it? Isn't it in-credible!"

Rizzoli nods; he can't believe the thunderous sound of it, then he hears a jockey saying, "JUST WORK HARD, SAVE, WORK HARD, SAVE" over and over again. *Nobody's jockey. Is the jockey . . . nineteenth-century?*

Now, after hearing the jockeys all urging their horses on, Rizzoli hears them fade away and the announcer's voice come back to say, "As they head for the far turn, it's Dream Killer still in the lead but losing ground as she steadily tosses away her inheritance. Ima Bright Boy moves up to second, inheriting the 150 million from the wife he murdered. Toscanini's Wig drops back to third, with Reality Therapy, who is tapping insurance funds as a new CEO, coming on strong. . . ."

"I shoulda bet Reality Therapy," Louie says to himself as Rizzoli watches Nobody Rules' little face moving along lost on the backstretch as the other seven faces race ahead, rounding the turn for the homestretch. *My horse is in the wrong race,* Rizzoli thinks just as he hears the announcer exclaim, "OH, NO! Ima Bright Boy has died of a heart attack at age forty-one pending his trial for his wife's murder. So, it's Dream Killer up front but NOW LOSING THE LEAD as she's passed on the outside by Reality Therapy and Toscanini's Wig. THESE TWO ARE NOSE TO NOSE FLAT OUT COMING OFF THE TURN INTO THE STRETCH! . . ."

Rizzoli watches Louie tense up, fidget and start to tear off tiny pieces of the racing form and throw them on the floor. They're both intent on the TV, watching this stretch run.

". . . REALITY THERAPY BY A NOSE. NO. TOSCANINI'S WIG BY A NOSE AND MORE. THEY'RE HEAD AND HEAD TO THE WIRE. WAIT! WAIT! COMING FROM NOWHERE IS, IS . . . IT'S NOBODY RULES. . . ."

My NOBODY?

". . . suddenly inheriting 100 million from a lost uncle's old mining claim turned valuable overnight. IT'S NOBODY RULES TAKING THE LEAD FROM TOSCANINI'S WIG AND DREAM THERAPY. NOBODY RULES WINS IT! CAN YOU BELIEVE OLD-FASHIONED PLUCK AND LUCK WINS IT AT THE WIRE, HORATIO ALGER STYLE!"

"ALL RIGHT!" Rizzoli exclaims, as Louie says, "SHIT!" There's a pause. "Wait," Louie says, "You had Nobody? You did?" Rizzoli nods. Louie hugs Rizzoli. "How much you put on him?"

"Two dollars," Rizzoli says. Louie starts laughing. "It's all I had," Rizzoli explains, getting a little angry that Louie seems to be making fun of him. "IT's ALL I HAD!"

"Your bill was . . . two hundred thousand," Louie says. "Not two dollars!"

TWO HUNDRED THOUSAND! NO! Rizzoli looks at his ticket. *YES, TWO HUNDRED THOUSAND AT 50 TO 1.* Rizzoli can't begin to fathom how much he just won. "Louie, what the hell, what can I do with it all? . . ."

"Rizzoli, the point is . . ."

"I wouldn't know what to spend it all on."

". . . point is . . . betting is just a way of killing time in Limbo. Money changes hands, but it doesn't mean anything. There's nothing to spend it on. In Limbo, we vegetate. No need to eat, have jobs. We just are. Not like down there where the race is."

Postscript

Concrete

Grace

....

A brisk early fall day. The taxi speeds on 57th. Rizzoli sits in the middle of the backseat, noticing the one green tree saved from these first cold nights. *Somehow.*

The taxi goes on. Rizzoli's head is down, engrossed in the *Times.*

He feels his taxi swing into the left lane and cut off the speeding car coming up behind.

His taxi slows. The car behind slows.

He keeps on reading as his taxi comes to a stop. *Probably for a stoplight.*

The car behind stops suddenly, close to his taxi's rear. Rizzoli keeps on reading.

"I saved her life."

"You what?" Rizzoli asks. Having been preoccupied, he glances up and sees the driver is looking at an ancient woman to the left of the front fender slowly crossing busy 57th in mid-block.

"I swerved into this lane to cut off that cab behind us. He was really coming."

The old woman gets to the other side of the street, never turning back, hunched over in her dark coat.

"You saved her life and she doesn't even know it."

"I know. I do it at least once a day," the driver says, starting off again. "I oughta have a counter here on the dashboard and for every pardoned life I save driving when they don't know, I'd punch it. Cabbies catch hell, but if they only knew."

Rizzoli imagines all the New Yorkers alive this very day who will never know they were saved by grace. *City grace.*

Rizzoli wonders if he were one of the ones who were saved and didn't know it.